I0709483

POODLES AND POISON

WHISKEY MYSTERY #2

In Your Face Ink LLC
9524 W. Camelback Road
#130-182
Glendale, AZ 85305
www.inyourfaceink.com
www.whiskeydogmysteries.com

First printed in the United States of America by In Your Face Ink LLC

Copyright © 2024 by In Your Face Ink LLC

All rights reserved.

This is a work of fiction. Names, characters, places, and incidents either are the product of the author's imagination or are used fictitiously, and any resemblance to actual persons, living or dead, businesses, companies, events, or locales is entirely coincidental.

ISBN: 978-0-9765659-9-4 (hardback)
ISBN: 978-1-7379733-5-5 (paperback)
ISBN: 978-1-7379733-6-2 (ebook)

Book design and cover by Rick Schank of Purple Couch Creative

*For Michelle Jacobson, our biggest fan and frequent asker of
"When's the next Whiskey dog book coming out?"
The answer is now. We love you.*

COMPENDIUM OF CLUES

CHAPTER ONE

On a late August Sunday in Cottageville with the sun shining overhead and a light breeze swaying the trees, Sarah Carter, owner of Carter's Canine Coiffure, wore a purple halter dress in honor of Oodle the poodle's collar color as she stood in Gladys Rossmiller's backyard. Sarah's Australian red heeler cattle dog Whiskey stood alert and somber at her feet like a guard at Buckingham Palace. The bald-headed grocer George, age unknown but Sarah thought was definitely over 65, was unlocking the front doors of Produce and More and called out, "Good morning, Sarah. The missus will bring Chutney by at eleven for a nail clipping."

Gladys was dressed in a black blouse and in black slacks, mirroring her grief. Tears trickled down her face as her neighbor and the owner of the local hardware store, Daniel Snyder, dug a hole between bushes in her rose garden. Thirty friends had gathered for the occasion of saying goodbye to Oodle and planting the urn with her ashes. No one knew exactly how old Oodle was when she went to her eternal sleep, but she and Gladys had been companions for more than two decades, and they belonged together the way Dalmatians did with firemen.

Sarah wiped a tear that slipped from her eye. Losing a beloved client was painful, and she and Whiskey, ever the empath, felt Gladys' grief like a tidal wave.

Wearing a black and white tweed suit—despite the summer heat—and sensible black shoes, Janice Jenkins, Sarah's next-door neighbor and Gladys' best friend, said a few words as the hole was dug. Janice was regaining her strength after surviving a kidnapping.

Chief James Order and his German shepherd Sascha were attending the service in Gladys' backyard. The chief held his hat over his heart and his eyes welled with unshed tears.

"Thank you all for gathering here today to remember Oodle," Janice said. "Oodle was a great poodle, and the perfect companion in Gladys' retirement, inspiring some of her best paintings."

The gathered friends smiled at that comment, and a few nodded their heads.

Janice continued, "Oodle was ever-present, loving, and a comfort to everyone, humans and other dogs alike. And we will miss her." She cleared her throat. "Would anyone like to share their favorite Oodle memory?" She looked around at all of the neighbors and their dogs, who were on their best behavior.

Daphne Smith, in a red maxi dress and a giant straw hat, held her French bulldog Pierre in one arm against her left side. She sniffed loudly before exclaiming, *"Je suis triste,"* and throwing the back of her right hand against her forehead and flicking outward in a dramatic gesture Sarah didn't understand.

"We all are," Sarah mumbled.

"C'est horrible," Daphne added. She got sidelong looks from some people. Everyone in Cottageville knew or knew of Daphne and her penchant for everything French, though she was a town native and had never been to France.

"It is very sad," Janice agreed. "Does anyone else want to share?"

Robert Wise, who lived on Sarah's block and was the music teacher at the local high school, said he and his students had created a song to honor Oodle. He snapped three times and launched into a jazzy number about unconditional love; soft, curly fur; comfort; canine companionship; and dog being God spelled backwards. The number was both comedic and heart-breaking at the same time, and Sarah wasn't sure if she should laugh or cry, so she did a bit of both.

At one very moving part three-quarters of the way through, Gladys dabbed her face with a lace handkerchief, and Whiskey left Sarah's side to offer his soft fur to Gladys to stroke. Sarah's heart-space warmed as she watched Whiskey tap Gladys' leg twice with his front paw. Gladys leaned from her chair and hugged him like a child does a new puppy.

From across the circle of people, Emily Colt, the Coiffure's assistant groomer, spoke up. Her hair was dyed purple today in honor of Oodle, and she wore a short black dress, tights, and black combat boots. "I loved how gentle and trusting Oodle was. Even when her cataracts clouded her vision, she still trusted us to trim her nails and bathe her and showed us love and never feared. We could learn from her." Emily's voice cracked on the last few words.

Sarah sent her a weak, but appreciative smile and a nod of her head. "I loved how she romped with Whiskey, and even when Oodle was older and slower, he could still get her going and bring out her inner puppy. It was beautiful to see," Sarah said.

"Yes, it was," Gladys agreed. "They were so good together." She wiped another tear from her cheek and ruffled Whiskey's fur with her crooked and swollen knuckled fingers.

Whiskey wiggled closer to her in response, and Gladys chuckled.

Sarah's best friend and owner of Java and Juice, Ginger said, "As Oodle aged, I had to find a biscuit recipe that was softer than what I usually make for the dogs that come in. Because of her, I learned a lot about senior dog health and nutrition. I will miss hearing her nails click on our café floor. May you rest in peace, Oodle. You brought a lot of comfort and joy into our lives. And for that, we are grateful."

Sarah saw Daniel smile at Ginger. Sarah was the only one in town who knew Daniel and Ginger had gone on a couple of dates and were trying to figure out what they were to each other. Town gossip spread faster than the global pandemic in 2020 so they were keeping seeing each other on the downlow. Ginger had grown up in Cottageville and known Daniel and his late wife all of her life.

Bill, a widower who sat every morning on his front porch with a gallon jar of dog biscuits while he read the newspaper and drank his coffee, said that he would miss seeing Gladys and Oodle walk past his house daily. "She didn't have enough teeth to eat the biscuits I buy, so sometimes I'd soak one in some chicken broth for her."

Gladys said, "I'll still come by, Bill. But I'd prefer coffee to a soggy biscuit." That made her friends and neighbors laugh.

Bill said, "Sure thing, Gladys."

Gladys smiled at him and then said, "I appreciate you all coming here today. I'm grateful for your love and support during this rough week. I know Oodle loved you all and I do, too. Daniel, if you'd be so kind to help this old lady..."

Daniel walked toward Gladys, but the chief got to her first. "Here, Gladys, I'll help you," Chief James said. He offered his elbow, and she put her arm through his.

He guided her across the lawn to the rose bushes, and Whiskey and Sascha followed them.

Daniel bent to the ground, picked up the urn, and held it toward Gladys.

She kissed the top of it and said, "Good dog." Tears ran rivulets down her cheeks. "I love you. Always." To Daniel she said, "I can't bend like I used to. Would you do the honors?"

In silence, Daniel crouched in front of the hole and placed the urn into it. Others in the yard crowded toward them, wanting to watch and to pay their final respects. Daniel scooped a hand spade of dirt and offered it to Gladys. The chief walked her another foot closer to the edge of the hole. She tilted the spade and watched the soil stream over the urn.

"Thank you," Gladys said, handing the spade back to Daniel. Her tears had stopped, and her blue eyes were clear, though slightly bloodshot. Then she turned, everyone backed up a step or two to give her room, and the chief escorted her back to her chair. But instead of sitting, she said, "A luncheon is inside. Please help yourself. Chief, if you could accompany me into the kitchen. I need a cup of tea."

"My pleasure," Chief James said. He guided Gladys up the back steps onto the small deck and into her house. Janice, Bill, Daphne, and most of the others followed.

But Sarah, Ginger, Emily, Sascha, and Whiskey stayed outside while Daniel covered the urn and filled in the hole. The vet's office had made a plaster imprint of Oodle's paw, and Gladys had asked Daniel to use that as a grave marker amongst the roses. Daniel pushed it into the dirt half an inch to make it secure. Whiskey sniffed the plaster marker once and then walked a few feet away before lifting his leg on a bush. Sarah rolled her eyes and thought, *At least he didn't mark the grave.*

"It's too bad Jared is away," Ginger said to Sarah. Ginger's blond curly hair framed her face instead of it being trapped in its usual ponytail or bun. Jared, Ginger's employee at the café, had been an integral part of Sarah's search for Mrs. Jenkins when she had disappeared. They had gone from having a joke-filled acquaintanceship to something more like a flirty friendship over the course of the summer. Sarah thought he would have appreciated the memorial service for Oodle, both for its quirkiness and because it brought a lot of the community together. Though Jared worked for Ginger at Java and Juice, his *real* vocation was writing and illustrating comic books and graphic novels, the latter of which he was shopping around to publishers. He was disappointed to miss the *Oodle fooneral*, as he called it, but he was in Vegas participating in Comic-Con. Over the last two days he had texted Sarah photos of people in all kinds of crazy costumes.

As Daniel and Ginger and Emily walked toward the back door of Gladys' house, Sarah whistled for Whiskey and Sascha to come. They had been sniffing the newly dug grave and then every bush on both sides of the marker.

The dogs raced past her as she said, "Slow down." They stopped on the deck and waited for her to catch up. And then they walked like the perfect gentle dogs they were into Gladys' house, before slurping up water from a bowl in her kitchen.

Sarah small-talked with people she knew, and she ate a cream cheese and cucumber finger sandwich and some potato salad. She cleared plates and cups and carried them from the living room and dining room into the kitchen. She was determined not to leave Gladys with a mess to clean up.

As she hand washed some china, Ginger popped into the kitchen and picked up a dish towel to dry what Sarah was washing. "Did Daniel leave?" Sarah asked.

"He had to go back to the store." Daniel had inherited Buck and Son from his father. They were the only hardware store in town and were open seven days a week. Ginger carefully dried the bowl Sarah handed her. "Do you know where this goes?"

"I believe it belongs in the breakfront in the dining room." Sarah picked up a plate from the counter and dunked it in the wash water.

Ginger left the room with the bowl. When she returned, she said, "Whiskey is curled up in a corner of the dining room. Almost everyone has left. Gladys and Janice are sitting on a sofa together talking. I'll start to bring the food in. Can you find some smaller containers?"

"Sure. Just let me finish this plate."

Twenty minutes later, Sarah and Ginger had all of the leftover food in smaller containers and stacked in Gladys' refrigerator. They had washed and dried all the casserole dishes and cake and sandwich stands and left them on the kitchen table since they weren't sure where they went. But the rest of the kitchen and the dining room were clean.

"Thank you," Sarah said.

"Of course." Ginger smiled. "It's what best friends do."

"What are you up to for the rest of the afternoon?" Sarah ran her hand through her ginger curls to push them out of her face.

"Daniel's coming over for dinner."

"Ooo la la," Sarah teased.

"It's going well, but we are taking it one date at a time."

"I don't see why," Sarah said. "You're both adults and know what you want. And that's not to be alone anymore. Makes sense to me." She winked at Ginger and then added, "Plus, he's a hard hunk of man. Why wouldn't you want that?"

Ginger laughed.

But Sarah understood not wanting to be alone. She had been for quite a while—moving to Cottageville from Seattle by herself more than six years ago and inheriting her grandmother's house. Sarah felt less alone since Whiskey had come into her life, but it wasn't the same as having a human partner.

Sarah wondered how long Gladys would wait before she went to the animal shelter and got another dog. Sarah knew the silence of losing a pet and living alone could be too loud.

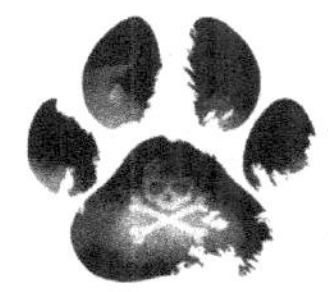

CHAPTER TWO

Later in the week as Sarah and Whiskey made their rounds around town during their morning walk before work, they found Gladys sitting next to Bill on his front porch. The newspaper was spread in front of him on the table, but they appeared deep in conversation.

Sarah didn't want to interrupt, so she waved her hand in greeting. But Whiskey climbed Bill's stairs and parked his butt next to Bill's chair, waiting for his treat.

"Whiskey, Sarah, so glad to see you this morning," Gladys said. "Sarah, I was going to stop by later, but since I see you now...well... would you accompany me to the poodle rescue tomorrow after you close the Coiffure for the day?"

"I'd be honored. Does that mean you want another companion?"

Gladys' eyes looked large and shiny behind her glasses. "Yes, dear. I know it is soon, but I'm not getting any younger and I don't like that I now find myself talking to myself." Gladys grinned. "At least with a dog around I can talk to him or her and don't look batty."

Bill cracked up at the comment. "It's as good a reason as any to get another dog." He reached into his big glass jar and pulled out a beef dog biscuit, asked Whiskey for his paw, and then gave the dog the biscuit after they shook for it.

"I'd take Bill with me," Gladys said, "but you know more about dogs. And I know you and Whiskey will help me pick a good one."

"We will certainly try. Did you set a time with them?"

"Six o'clock. Is that okay?"

"It is."

"I will drive us. I'll swing by at 5:45 and pick you up. Thank you, dear." Gladys picked up her coffee mug and took a sip.

"My pleasure," Sarah said, waving for Whiskey to get off the porch and to come with her.

A few minutes later, Sarah pushed open the red door on Java and Juice which caused the bell above the door to jingle. Three people were in line in front of Jared, so Sarah eyed the pastry case noticing that the muffin of the day was banana walnut, the donuts were glazed, and the tarts were either lemon curd or raspberry. The case also contained the usual assortment of croissants, eclairs, and cinnamon and sugar-covered crullers. Her stomach rumbled like it demanded one of everything.

Sarah turned to walk to the end of the line and was surprised to find Whiskey already holding their place. "Smart dog," she said, rubbing his head between his ears. He knew he'd receive a homemade chicken biscuit as soon as it was his turn in front of Jared.

And sure enough, Jared smiled and said, "Whiskey, my man," and reached over the counter to high five Whiskey's right front paw. Then he tossed the biscuit into the air and Whiskey popped up to catch it with the enthusiasm of snagging a fly ball to win the World Series.

"Mi'lady," Jared said to Sarah, and he bowed from his waist in mock chivalry. "What can I get for her royal highness today?" He reached for her empty to-go coffee mug so it could be filled with their house blend black coffee.

"Two barbeque chicken salads, one each of the tarts, and a cruller, my lord." Sarah held her hands on the edges of an imaginary skirt and curtsied.

"A feast fit for a lady...or two." Jared's blue eyes sparkled.

Sarah ran her credit card through the machine on the counter, adding a healthy twenty-five percent tip for Jared, and then reached for her go-cup and the bag with her food. "I'm glad you are back," she said quietly.

"Me, too," Jared said. "I'll text you later."

"Sounds good."

Suddenly a thump came from a corner table and Sarah turned to see what had happened. A man she didn't know hit the table again with his fist as his face turned purple. From his throat came wheezes like a St. Bernard with emphysema.

"Call nine-one-one," Sarah said, racing toward the man's table, with Whiskey by her side.

"Are you choking?" she asked, putting her stuff on his table, before getting behind him to start the Heimlich maneuver. She pumped her fist into his stomach once and then again and again, but nothing came out and his wheezing got worse.

Ginger and Jared were both at the table now. "Choking or an allergy?" Ginger asked.

The man's eyes bugged like a pug's at Ginger's question.

She turned and looked around her café. "Anyone have an epi-pen?"

No one responded.

Within five minutes the front door pushed open, the bell tinkled, and Wendy and Walter Parks, the town's volunteer paramedics, rushed in carrying a bag of medical supplies and pushing a stretcher. They were followed by Officer John Beams.

The man's hands were now on his throat as he struggled to breathe. Wendy pulled out a liquid-filled syringe and jammed the needle into the man's thigh. His whole body went rigid, and his eyes widened before he released an audible breath. The man noisily sucked air into his body before forcing it back out. In and out, in and out.

"Here, let's give you some oxygen to help elevate your saturation levels," Walter said. He pulled out a silicone oxygen mask that had hosing attached to a small tank.

"I'll be fine," the man rasped, shaking his head no.

"We have to take you in for an evaluation," Walter insisted. "All of that epinephrine can save your life, but the symptoms can return when it wears off."

The man, who Sarah guessed was in his fifties, gave Walter a hard stare.

"I'm serious," Walter said. "Plus, you may need additional treatment."

Wendy pushed the rolling bed closer to the table. "Hop on and we'll give you a free ride." She smiled at the man.

Officer Beams stepped forward and guided the man to standing with a hand on his elbow. The man said nothing but climbed aboard, and Walter slipped the mask over his face.

Barbara Order, the chief's wife who had been sitting at a table by the door with her best friend, stood and opened the door for the Parks and the stretcher.

Once they were safely outside and loading the man into the ambulance, Officer Beams said, "Anyone want to tell me what happened? Sarah? Ginger?" He pulled out a chair at the table, sat, and motioned for them to do the same. Jared walked back to his position at the register, and the rest of the café resumed what they had been doing before the drama.

Sarah said, "I didn't notice the man, really, until he pounded his hand on the table. Then I realized he was in trouble. But I thought he choked so I started the compressions on his diaphragm."

Ginger picked up, "But that wasn't working, and the man was gasping like a fish out of water and seemed to be getting worse. That's when I realized he could be having an allergic reaction, so I asked if anyone had an injector."

"And that's when Wendy and Walter came in. And you," Sarah finished.

Officer Beams had pulled a small tablet out of his pocket and made a few notes. "What did he purchase?" He looked at the table and the muffin crumbs sticking to the paper wrapper and the empty cappuccino cup.

Ginger looked toward Jared and asked, "Muffin, cap, anything else?"

Jared said, "Cappuccino with hemp milk, banana walnut muffin, ham and cheese croissant sandwich. Oh, and he bought an orange."

Sarah, Ginger, and Officer Beams looked at the tabletop. There was no sign of the orange. *Weird. Had he put it in his pocket?* Sarah stuck her head under the bistro table and looked at the wooden floor. *Had it fallen off when he banged the table?*

"Does anyone see an orange on the floor?" she asked over the din.

People glanced under their tables and around the room. But no one said, "I see an orange."

Jared held up an orange from a basket on the counter and called Whiskey. "Whiskey, see this? Go get it. Where is it, boy?" Whiskey ran to Jared and sniffed the orange that Jared held in front of his nose.

Whiskey thumped his red and white tail enthusiastically then zigged one way across the café and then the other sniffing here and sniffing there.

The café patrons encouraged him by patting his head as he came past or saying, "Good boy. Where is it?" Or "Go, Whiskey, find the orange."

He wiggled his nose along the baseboard of one wall all of the way to the bathroom door before jerking his head up, giving one sharp bark, and scratching the door with his paw.

Officer Beams got up and opened the bathroom door for Whiskey and followed behind him. When they re-emerged, John had an orange in his hand, and the dog walked with the confidence of Beyonce at his side. "It was in the trash can. He went right to it."

The café erupted into claps. Sarah hugged her cattle dog, and Ginger gave him a second biscuit.

Officer Beams bagged the orange. "I'm not sure why this was in the trash, but since that seems suspicious, and we still aren't sure what happened—"

"Or even who that man is," Sarah added.

John Beams smiled at her. "Yes, that too. I'm taking this with me." To Ginger he said, "I'll be back if I need more information."

"Of course," Ginger said, and then added more to herself than to anyone else, "Though I don't know why you'd order things you might be allergic to."

Officer Beams approached the counter. "Jared, did he ask about any ingredients in what he ordered?"

"No. Not at all. He asked if we had hemp milk, saying he preferred it or oat, but we ran out of oat milk earlier this morning."

"Okay. While I'm here, can I get a black coffee to go?"

"Sure thing." Jared poured the coffee into a tall paper cup and eyed Ginger before saying, "It's on the house."

"Bribing an officer after poisoning someone, are you?" Officer Beams joked.

"I would never," Jared insisted, his grin flashing his top row of teeth.

Sarah and Whiskey left Java and Juice with Officer Beams. "What a way to start the day," Sarah said as they were walking down the sidewalk. "I hope that man will be okay."

"I'll follow up with him at the hospital. Thank you, Sarah, for your quick thinking on the Heimlich."

"Even if it wasn't necessary." Sarah smiled.

"You never know," John said. "Have a good day." He unlocked the cruiser parked at the curb.

Sarah and Whiskey walked two more blocks to Carter's Canine Coiffure, which had already been unlocked and set up for the day by Emily. Sarah set the breakfast food and her coffee on the counter and put their salads in the fridge in the back room of the converted house. Emily's purple hair had been teased into spikes and she wore a bone-patterned apron over a black rock concert t-shirt and jeans.

Sarah grabbed a cartoon corgi apron from a hook and tied it around her waist. "It's been quite a morning." She launched into the story about the man at the café.

"Have you seen him around here before?" Emily asked as Sergio's two shelties Sean and Sophia pranced through the door followed by Sergio himself. Whiskey greeted the shelties with a sniff and he licked Sophia's ear. "Here," Sergio said, thrusting the leashes at Sarah. "Barbara is blowing up my phone. I'm five minutes late for her color. But the kids didn't want to cooperate this morning. They were like oooh, we have to smell this and oooh, we have to smell that." He threw up his hands like he was over it.

Sarah laughed. "Dogs will be dogs. We'll have them ready by lunchtime. I saw Barbara this morning, and I'm sure she hates that her roots are showing."

"You have no idea," Sergio said, before turning and trouncing through the door.

Emily laughed. "Cottageville drama. Now back to the man. So, you saved his life—"

"Probably Wendy did."

"But you have no idea who he is."

"Nope. He wore a white short-sleeve dress shirt and black dress pants."

Emily cut in, "So he dressed like a Mormon on his mission?"

The remark surprised Sarah, but when she thought for a split second, she realized that yes, the man was dressed as she had seen many Mormon missionaries dress. "Yes, though he was much older than mission age. I'd say mid-fifties."

"So, they took him away in the ambulance?"

"Yes. Apparently once you are injected with epinephrine you have to seek emergency medical care."

"Good to know," Emily said, starting the water and scooping up Sean. "I'll wash this one today and you wash Sophia."

"Okay. Oh, and Gladys asked me to go with her to look at rescue poodles tomorrow night. Isn't that sweet?"

"Wow. Moving on already. Good for her."

Sarah started the water and put Sophia in the tub. Whiskey sat at her feet watching his friends get their baths and being groomed, until he was distracted by Officer John Beams walking through the Coiffure front door.

CHAPTER THREE

Whiskey beelined to the front door and greeted Officer Beams with a wagging tale and a friendly woof.

"Hello, Whiskey. Nice to see you again."

Sarah finished clipping the last of Sophia's toenails, and then took her off the table and placed her on the floor. "I'll be right back," she said to the sable sheltie.

As she approached the front room, Sarah joked, "We meet again...and so soon."

"Sorry to interrupt the beginning of your workday, but the chief thought it would be good to swing by and check on you. Giving someone the Heimlich maneuver is very stressful, plus you watched the man almost die, so we wanted to make sure you are okay."

Taken aback because she hadn't emotionally processed all the details of the morning yet, Sarah said, "I think so. Honestly, I arrived here at work and have been busy, so other than telling Emily about it, I haven't thought much about it."

"I understand. Well, if you need to talk to someone, we have counselors available through the department," said Officer Beams.

Looking into his hazel eyes, Sarah saw a compassion that she'd never noticed before. "I appreciate the offer, John, but I am sure I will be fine. If the whole ordeal with Mrs. Jenkins didn't shake me, I doubt what happened this morning will."

"Good point, Sarah. You are tough, that's for sure."

"Girl power!" Emily yelled from behind the counter where she was brushing Sean as he stood on a stainless steel table. His sister sat on Emily's Doc Marten and stretched her neck looking up at them.

Sarah and Officer Beams laughed.

"I know I already took your statement earlier, but can we sit down and go over the details again?"

"Sure." To Emily, Sarah raised her voice and said, "I'll be a few more minutes."

"No problem. Everything all right?"

"I think so."

Sarah and Officer Beams sat in the waiting area and rehashed the details from the café. Sarah reiterated that nothing seemed abnormal until the man started banging his fist on the table.

"Everything happened so fast," Sarah exclaimed. "I was performing the Heimlich, but his wheezing got worse. Then the next thing I know, the front door flew open, and the Parks rushed in carrying a bag of medical supplies and pushing the stretcher. Then you walked in right behind them."

"Yes, I arrived on the scene right as they were about to enter Java and Juice."

"How did you all get there so fast? Who called nine-one-one?"

Officer Beams furrowed his brows, and his eyes widened reminding Sarah of a surprised pug.

"That is a very good question, Sarah. Who did call nine-one-one? There is no way we would have arrived at Java and Juice if you were just starting to administer the Heimlich maneuver."

"I know. Right. I yelled 'someone call nine-one-one' when the man thumped on the table, and I ran toward him. We live in a small town, but unless you and the Parks have the Flash's superpowers, it would have been impossible to get there almost before I said to make the call. You aren't telepathic, right?" Sarah grinned.

Officer Beams smiled and Sarah noticed his teeth looked like they had been recently whitened. "No, not telepathic. I'm with you. Something doesn't make sense."

"What are you thinking?" Sarah's investigative mind buzzed like a disturbed beehive.

"When I go back to the station, I'll talk to dispatch and see when the call came in. They should also be able to tell me what number the call was made from. I think that's the best place to start."

"Okay. Sounds good." Sarah nodded her head causing her ginger ponytail to bounce.

"Thanks, Sarah. I will let you know what I find out."

As John Beams started toward the door, he told Sarah that the chief was at the high school meeting with the principal because a fight broke out after school yesterday that led to a retaliation this morning, a broken windshield in the school parking lot.

"Oh no, I hope no one was hurt."

"The two teenagers who fought yesterday were pretty banged up, but no one was in the car this morning when the hockey team captain took one of his old sticks to the captain of the football team's Honda Civic."

Shaking her head in disbelief, Sarah said, "What's wrong with kids these days?"

"In my opinion, they see too much violence on social media and the internet, so they become numb to it. Almost like they forget that the things they see in the movies and in videos can't be acted out in real life because they will cause pain and death."

Intrigued by John's response, Sarah said, "I bet in your line of work you see it more and more every year."

"It's true. And not just more violence, but we see younger and younger children committing violent crimes. Anyway, I could talk all day about this subject, but I gotta get back to the station."

"Okay. Thanks for checking in on me, I appreciate it."

"You bet, Sarah. I'll let the chief know you are fine. See ya."

Officer Beams exited the Coiffure's green front door and Sarah hurried to the back to help Emily.

"Emily, did you know there was a fight at the high school yesterday?"

"Yeah, I saw a stream of it on IG Reels last night. It was a good fight, too. Both the kids practice that mixed martial arts stuff."

Intrigued, Sarah asked "What classifies a fight as a good fight, Em?"

"They kicked, punched, and wrestled. It looked like one of them might have gotten his nose broken."

Rolling her eyes, Sarah mumbled, "Officer Beams was right."

"What did you say?"

"Nothing."

Brushing Sophia's beautiful brown and white fur, Sarah explained that there was no way that the Parks and the police could have arrived on the scene at Java and Juice as fast as they did, unless they were called before the situation started. She told Emily that Officer Beams was going to talk to dispatch to see what time the call was placed and from what number.

"Weird," Emily said. "Hey, did I tell you we are reading *The Hounds of Baskerville* in my lit class?"

"No. Have you watched *Sherlock*?"

"Loved it. That was in season two."

"Yep. It was a bit creepy." Sarah shivered like a scared chihuahua.

Emily smiled and said, "Yes, it was gothic. So cool."

Sarah's mind wandered to the timing of things at the café. What would have happened if the Parks hadn't arrived when they did?

Emily and Sarah finished both shelties' complete spa treatment and tied a blue bandana around Sean's neck and a red bandana around Sophia's. They looked adorable, even though the blue and red bandanas were more of a July fourth vibe. The women scooped up the Shetland sheepdogs under their bellies and placed them on the floor. Whiskey jumped to his feet and began to play with his two friends.

As Sarah broomed loose fur into a dustpan, she said, "Hey, don't get dirty and mess up those bandanas. You know how particular your human is."

Emily laughed aloud. "Isn't that the truth."

Sarah pulled her cell phone out of the front pocket of her apron and called Ginger. It rang and rang, and eventually went to her voicemail. Sarah didn't feel like leaving a message, so she hung up and tried Jared's number.

On the third ring Jared answered with, "Hello. mi'lady."

"Good day, my lord. I tried calling Ginger, but she didn't answer."

"Oh, I see how it is. Now I'm a second-rate friend. Thanks a lot." Jared snickered.

Laughing into the phone, Sarah said, "Come on, you know that's not true."

"If it's not true, then you can prove it by going to dinner with me one night this week."

"Are you asking me out on a date?" Sarah's smile was as big as a quokka's.

"Wait, what?" Emily stood frozen holding wet towels over the washing machine. Her eyebrows were raised.

"I believe so, Sarah. And I promise to be on my best Cottageville behavior."

"I'm not sure what that means, but I gladly accept your invitation to dinner." Changing the subject before it became awkward,

Sarah explained that she called to check in on Ginger and make sure she was okay after this morning's stress.

But before Jared answered, Sarah received an incoming call from John Beams. "Jared, I gotta go. Officer Beams is calling me. Talk soon."

Hitting the end call and then the answer button, Sarah said, "Hello, Officer Beams."

"Hey, Sarah, I talked to dispatch, so they will review the call log and run the number. Chief Order texted and said that he's going to go to the hospital to check on our John Doe once he is finished at the high school. Maybe before the day is over, we will find out more details."

"Thanks for the update, John, talk to you later."

Sarah hung up and was surprised by the time. "It's almost eleven. Wow. Where did the morning go?"

No sooner had the words left Sarah's lips, when the front door opened, and Tony and Spike entered the Coiffure.

As if he was the Pied Piper of shelties, Whiskey, followed by Sean and Sophia, made his way to the waiting area to greet Tony, a monster-sized bodybuilder who owned Big T's Fitness Center, and Spike, his seventy-five-pound pit bull, who looked just like his human.

Sarah popped through the movable opening in the top of the Coiffure's front counter and greeted Tony and Spike. "Good Lord, Tony. Every time you come in you have new muscles popping out somewhere. You're like a cane corso now."

Laughing, Tony said, "Thank you. I'll take that as a compliment."

"I mean I don't understand the whole bodybuilding thing, and honestly, I'm not even sure how you get muscles that big, but I know you work hard at it, so you should take pride in the results, right?"

"Yes. And thank you. I've been cutting down on size the past few months because we have a photo shoot tomorrow, so I need to be more defined for the pictures. We are launching a new supplement line and our marketing agent wants Spike to be with me in the pictures. He says having my dog in the pictures will help us connect with people outside our normal demographic."

"Sounds like you have a wise marketing agent."

"I sure hope so. He costs an arm and a leg, that's for sure."

"Do you have to pay with fewer arms and legs, since yours are so big?" Sarah joked.

With a huge grin, Tony replied, "That's pretty funny, Sarah."

Sarah knew that Tony worked extremely hard on his business as well as his physique. She had heard people gossip that he was a dumb meathead, but she knew that was the furthest thing from the truth. Tony earned an MBA from The Wharton School at the University of Pennsylvania, and he volunteered as a mentor for troubled youth at the Finding Hope Center on Gladkins Street.

"What can we do for Spike today?" asked Sarah. "I don't think I have any spiked collars to put on him after he's groomed."

Tony chuckled. "That's okay, I have plenty of them at home. Spike needs to look good for the photo shoot, so give him the complete spa package. The one with nail trimming and please, brush his teeth well for me, too. He hates when I brush his teeth."

"Okay, we will have Spike looking like Mr. T in no time. And

I don't mean you, Mr. Tony, I mean the original Mr. T."

"You are full of one-liners today, Sarah."

"I guess I'm in a weird mood. It's been a crazy day and it's only eleven o'clock."

Emily appeared from the back room, greeted Tony, and interrupted the dogs' playtime long enough to grab Spike by his collar and guide him to the back. "I think Spike weighs more than I do."

"He better not because I have had him cutting with me for the photo shoot."

"Alrighty, Big T," said Sarah. "We will have Spike ready for you to pick up around two."

"Sounds good. Thanks." Tony left as Sarah made her way into the back.

Emily wore a smirk and said, "Really, Sarah. 'Do you have to pay with fewer arms and legs, since yours are so big?' Since when do you flirt with customers, especially customers that large and muscular?"

"Are you serious right now? I wasn't flirting with Tony. He is so not my type."

Emily shook her head. "I've known you for almost two years, and I know how you are around dudes, and that my friend, was flirting. I actually thought for a moment that you were going to be bold enough to ask him for his handle on Only Fans."

"Eww, no. Em, you are a weirdo!"

"You know you were thinking about those huge arms pulling you against his rock-hard shaven chest."

"Emily Colt, what is wrong with you? And besides, it's not the rock-hard chest, it's the six-pack abs that gets to me. And how do you know he shaves his chest?"

Emily and Sarah both had a good laugh before Sarah interjected, "Remember you little eavesdropper, I have a date with Jared this week."

"Eavesdropper. Those are fighting words, girl. How could I not hear you when this place is small?"

Sarah smiled. "Good point. I'm going to text Sergio and let him know his furry companions are finished and ready to be picked up."

The suds overflowed from Spike's bath water, as Emily shampooed the pit bull's short, fine-textured fur. For a larger, aggressive looking dog, Spike was very mild-mannered and well behaved.

"Hey Em, good news. Sergio is sending Travis over to retrieve the shelties."

Emily narrowed her eyes at Sarah. "And why is that good news?"

"Come on, Emily, not too long ago you stayed up all night texting Travis *and* Taylor. Don't tell me you stopped crushing on him already."

"Man, you are salty today. You know I think Travis is hot, but just because I think he's hot doesn't mean I've got a thing for him."

"Oh, I get it. He's eye candy, but that's it. Actually, if I were to stereotype, which I wouldn't, I might think Travis is gay."

"Here we go. Please Sarah, since you aren't stereotyping, enlighten me with your keen observations."

"Travis is always dressed to the hilt, like he is off the pages of *GQ*. His laundered black pants and black shirts must arrive every morning directly from the cleaners. Every day his precision-cut wavy chestnut hair is molded perfectly in place and his mannerisms and vocabulary are refined like a Harvard Scholar."

With a giant smirk, Emily said, "So those characteristics cause you to think that Travis could be gay? You do know that Taylor wears black clothes every day too, right?"

Sarah's cheeks turned a soft shade of pink as she blushed and shrugged her shoulders. "Emily, I like Taylor, but Taylor looks like Johnny Deep in *Edward Scissorhands* and Travis resembles Brad Pitt in *Ocean's Eleven*. All I was saying is that Taylor dresses and acts like some of the gay friends I ran around with in Seattle. They were hot and they dressed impeccably."

"Good thing you clarified that you weren't stereotyping, Sarah, because it sure seems to me like you were. You are something else today. What did Jared put in your coffee this morning? If I didn't know you, I would think you are micro dosing shrooms."

"Maybe I am. Maybe I snuck some out of your backpack."

"Please, Ms. Sassy, just cause I'm in college doesn't mean I do college girl things."

Noticing Spike's bulging muscles as she was washing the lather out his fur, Emily changed the subject. "Sarah, look at Spike's muscles. Do you think Tony trains him?"

"He's a beast, that's for sure. I did hear Tony say one time that he puts a homemade weight vest on Spike and puts him on the treadmill at the gym. I'm not sure if it's a publicity stunt or if Spike actually works out. But he definitely looks like a canine version of a professional bodybuilder."

Whiskey, Sean, and Sophia were chasing each other through the Coiffure, so Sarah squatted down to their level, spoke to them in a tone like they were small children and reminded them to calm down.

"Why is it we seem to have canines that resemble us, Sarah?"

Smiling and showing her beautiful white, straight teeth, the results of two years and three months of braces, Sarah said, "You aren't referring to Spike and Tony, are you?"

With a snort laugh, Emily responded, "Now what would make you think that?"

Both Sarah and Emily chuckled for a bit before Sarah said, "There is some sort of psychology behind it. Meaning that it doesn't simply happen by chance. I read in *Dogs Naturally* that this phenomenon is referred to as the mere exposure effect. We humans tend to choose things that are familiar, so we select our canine companion because of a preference for the familiar. And Em, if you don't believe all that psychobabble, then the real reason is because we are narcissists."

Emily shook her head in playful disbelief to what Sarah was saying.

Sarcastically bantering with Emily, Sarah walked over to Spike and put her left arm around his thick, wet neck, "Hey Spikey, look at Emily and tell her you don't look like Tony. Go ahead, tell her."

Emily stopped scrubbing Spike for a moment and put her towel over the edge of the bath basin and stood with her right hand on her hip, looking at Sarah. Her eyes were narrowed and her mouth was a straight line.

Sarah continued, "Look Spike, Emily doesn't think I'm funny."

Emily reached into Spike's bath water, cupped shampoo suds in both hands, and laughingly threw them on Sarah.

Both women began scooping bath suds into their hands and

threw them at each other. Whiskey raced to them and barked once like he wasn't about to miss out on the fun. He stood up on his hind legs, with his front paws on the bathtub, and attempted to retrieve suds with his nose, but he couldn't reach. The shelties yapped at his heels.

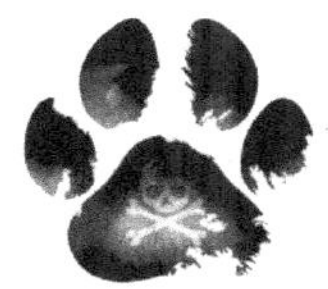

CHAPTER FOUR

s the commotion continued in the back room, Sean and Sophia left the excitement when the front door opened and the bell over the door chimed.

That chime caused Sarah to dump her handful of suds back into the tub. She headed toward the front of the Coiffure. "Come on, Whiskey, let's go see who it is."

She passed through the opening in the counter and said, "Hey Travis, how are you?"

Squatting down to their level, Travis greeted the shelties he was there to retrieve. He looked up at her and his eyes went wide in what Sarah assumed was surprised as she realized she was dripping water and soap. "Hello Sarah, I am fine. Thank you. How are you?"

"I'm well. Emily and I were just having a little fun in the back grooming room."

"I guess that explains the shampoo suds in your hair."

"Oops, yes. I didn't realize I had suds in my hair," responded Sarah.

"I am sure that you and Emily have a lot of fun together. I like my job, but we do not have fun." Smiling and revealing his pearly teeth, Travis continued, "Could you imagine Sergio greeting a client with shampoo suds in his hair?"

Laughing and shaking her head no, Sarah admitted, "I don't think I could picture Sergio with anything in his hair other than products."

"So true, Sarah, so true."

Yelling hello from the back room, Emily greeted Travis and told him he was welcome to join them anytime in a back room suds throwing competition.

Travis stood up and took the liberty to step past the front counter and poked his head through the archway into the back room to see Emily.

"Hey Em, what's up?"

"Nothing really. It's been a pretty chill day here so far...except for a little suds throwing."

Travis eyed the large pit bull and said, "Holy cow, that dog must be on steroids."

Almost in unison, Emily and Sarah, who was now back in the grooming area, said, "If you think Spike is muscular, you should see his human."

"There's a human version of Spike in town?" asked Travis.

Emily said, "Why yes, Travis, and according to world renown dog psychologist Dr. Sarah Carter, this beautiful canine was chosen by his human because of the phenomenon referred to as the mere exposure effect."

"I didn't know you earned a doctorate, Sarah. Congratulations."

"I do not have a doctorate; Emily is being Emily right now. She's such a little smart—"

Emily interjected before Sarah said her final word. "I want to test Dr. Carter's hypothesis. Are you ready?"

Sarah and Travis smiled and acknowledged that they were.

"Okay then, in your expert opinions, do Sophia and Sean resemble Sergio?"

Travis looked confused.

Emily, having the patience of a race car driver revving their engine at the starting line, blurted out, "I'm waiting."

Smiling, yet a little uneasy, Travis said, "I know this may be just semantics, but is the question does Sergio resemble his shelties, or is the question, do the shelties resemble Sergio?"

Emily shook her head, which had no effect on her purple hair. "There is one in every bunch. Whichever way you'd like to consider the question is fine by me, just answer the fricking question."

"If Sergio ever finds out I said this, I'm a dead man."

All three of them chuckled and Travis continued, "The shelties are pretty like Sergio, they like to be pampered and doted on like Sergio, and oddly enough, their eating habits are similar to his. All three of them only eat organic, nitrate-free foods."

Following Travis' lead, Sarah said, "I agree. There are very strong similarities. In fact, I would go as far as to say their gaits are similar, in the way they walk with a high-society air as well as the way they sit, which is very prim and proper."

"And this, ladies and gentlemen, is another reason I will not have a canine," Emily said. "I do not want people telling me how much I look or act like my dog. That's so not cool."

The three of them laughed and Sarah acknowledged Emily's wittiness, but she responded, "You'd look better with an iguana anyway."

Before Emily responded, the bell on the front door chimed and in walked Lilly, a one-hundred-twenty-pound harlequin great Dane, followed by Lisa and Holly, Lilly's humans. Whiskey raced from Sophia and Sean and slid to a stop next to Lilly. Whiskey didn't get to see Lilly that often, but when he did, he acted like a middle school boy around a very cute thirteen-year-old girl. He even seemed a bit tongue-tied as he didn't even offer a vocal greeting.

Sarah scurried out from the back room to greet their guests. "Hello, ladies. How are you?"

Lisa wore hiking boots, faded blue jeans, and a black pocketless t-shirt, and her wife was dressed similarly but in shorts. Sarah wondered if they had been trekking through the woods around their bed and breakfast and birding as they often did.

Almost in unison, Holly and Lisa responded that they were doing well and that they were enjoying the August weather.

"It is beautiful, for sure. How are things at Whispering Pines?"

Lisa responded, "This has been the best quarter we've had since opening the Boutique."

Holly said, "We've actually doubled our revenue from last year."

"That's great. What helped bring in the new customers?"

Lisa extended her index finger and pointed at Holly, "It was all her."

Blushing and leaning into Lisa, Holly said, "It was nothing really. We advertised on some of the larger, pet-friendly travel platforms and offered a nice cash incentive for referrals that booked directly with us on our web page."

"Holly says it's nothing, but this little marketing genius of mine doubled our revenue in less than a year."

Sarah said, "That's quite impressive. Maybe I should hire you to do our marketing, too."

A splash came from the back, and the women heard Emily's voice. "Come on, Spike, please cooperate. I haven't finished rinsing you yet." She yelled for Sarah to come help.

"I can help, Em," said Travis. He started rolling up the sleeves of his black shirt.

"You are too pretty. You will get wet," Emily said.

Sarah said, "Excuse me. I need to check on Emily." Entering the back room, Sarah found Emily sprawled over the tub and on top of Spike. Travis was standing by helplessly. "What in the world are you doing?"

"Spike has been trying to jump down out of the bath to visit with Whiskey and Lilly, so I've been doing everything I can to keep him in the tub."

Chuckling, Sarah said, "I should take a picture of this and send it to Tony and show him what we really do at Carter's Canine Coiffure."

Turning toward Travis, Sarah smiled. "Is this what Sergio does with unruly women at the sink?"

Emily rolled her eyes and kept all her weight on Spike. "Very funny, Sarah. Ha ha."

Sarah helped Emily take Spike out of the warm bath water and onto the grooming table, before returning to the front of the shop to retrieve Lilly and give Holly and Lisa a send-off.

Interrupting Whiskey's and Lilly's flirtatious play, Sarah said to Lilly, "Say goodbye to your humans."

As Sarah turned and started leading Lilly back to the grooming area, she said over her shoulder that Lilly would be ready by three.

In the grooming area, she said, "Emily, do you realize that between these two dogs, they probably weigh over two hundred pounds."

"Oh, I know. Trust me. My arms and shoulders are going to feel it tonight."

"For sure. Good thing we've only had the shelties this morning and not Sascha or Sebastian the St. Bernard."

Realizing he needed to return to the salon, Travis started to roll his sleeves back down. "Sarah, can I pay before you get started on Lilly?"

"Are things too exciting for you at Carter's Canine Coiffure?" Sarah teased.

"No, I actually like it here, but Sergio is a stickler on how long errands should take, even when I am doing them for him."

"Control freak," Emily's voice boomed.

Travis nodded. "Yeah, you could say that."

Holding onto Lilly's collar and trying to convince Whiskey to sit down in the corner of the shop, Sarah said to Travis, "Sergio still hasn't used the Loyal Customer Coupon that we gave him a few months ago, so today's visit will be two-hundred dollars even."

Travis reached into his front left pants pocket and counted out three, one-hundred-dollar bills and told Sarah that Sergio said she'd say that. He then told her the extra was a tip.

Still holding onto Lilly with her left hand, Sarah accepted the money with her right and proceeded to slide it into the front pocket of her apron. "Tell Sergio we said thank you."

Travis squatted down and connected the shelties' leashes to their collars, thanked Sarah, awkwardly said bye to Emily, then headed past the front counter and out the front door.

"Not a word, Sarah. Not a word." Emily insisted before Sarah could say otherwise.

"Em, is eye-candy one word or is it two?"

"Shut it, Sarah, or I will sic Spike on you."

Sarah was opening her mouth to say something, but she was interrupted by the bell on the front door notifying them that they had another visitor.

Letting go of Lilly, Sarah said, "Come on, dogs, let's see who it is."

Whiskey was the first at the door to greet Chief James. Lilly sniffed his waist and gun holster, which is where her head naturally hit.

"Hey, Chief."

"Hello, Sarah. Whose big dog is this? I don't think I have seen her around town."

"That is Lilly. Her humans are Lisa and Holly, the owners of Whispering Pines Boutique Bed and Breakfast."

"Oh yeah, that's right. I just don't remember her being so big."

"She's over one-hundred-twenty pounds for sure," said Sarah.

Looking down at Lilly and rubbing her between the ears with one hand and stroking Whiskey's neck with his other hand, the chief said, "She's a big one!"

Sarah smiled and agreed. "I've heard you've had a busy day."

"Yes, it's been quite a day already. I dealt with the school situation by meeting with the teenagers, their parents, and the principal, then I went to the hospital to check on our John Doe, whose actual name is Richard Clarkson."

"Richard Clarkson." Sarah repeated. "I've never seen him before, and I have not heard that name around here."

"Yeah, that makes two of us. And believe it or not, I know most people in our small town. Or at least I recognize their names."

Sarah looked Chief James in the eyes when she asked, "What else did you find out about him?"

"Honestly, not much at this point. We have his name, know he was passing through town, and stopped for breakfast at Java and Juice…"

Sarah interrupted the chief, "What about the orange allergy?"

"That's an interesting question. According to doctors, there are orange allergies, and there are citric acid allergies, and they are not one in the same. However, both can cause a rash, tingling on the lips and in the throat, and in the worst-case scenario, vomiting. Neither allergy causes the symptoms that Richard Clarkson exhibited."

"So, he didn't really have an allergic reaction?" asked Sarah.

"Oh, he definitely did, but to what is the million-dollar question."

"The whole ordeal doesn't make sense, Chief. This Clarkson guy almost died at Java and Juice from an allergic reaction, somehow the Parks and Officer Beams arrived at the café while I performed the Heimlich on him, then, after he was taken away on a stretcher, Officer Beams and Whiskey found his orange in the bathroom's trash can. I may not be Inspector Clouseau, but things don't add up."

"I am with you, and it doesn't take Inspector Clouseau's experience to recognize that things don't make sense. Plus, Mr. Clarkson's mouth is shut tighter than a clam holding a precious pearl. The only thing I got out of him was his name, his address, and that he must have had an allergic reaction to something he ate, so that's usually an indication that there is more to this than what meets the eye...or the ear in this case."

Whiskey and Lilly left the chief's side and wrestled with each other in between Sarah and Chief James as they talked. Emily yelled from the back room, "Sarah, you gotta do something about those two. Spike can't handle being left out, and I can't blow dry him and hold him on the table at the same time."

Crouching down, Sarah grabbed Whiskey and pulled him close to her legs, while the chief grabbed Lilly and struggled to pull her huge body closer to his.

"What about the orange? Is someone running tests on it?"

"The orange is being sent off to the lab, but since there isn't a crime scene or any criminal activity that we know of, it won't be processed as 'urgent' so it could be a few days or even a couple of weeks until we have any results."

"Are you kidding? Sure seems to be something criminal going on," exclaimed Sarah.

Standing up and letting go of Lilly, the chief said, "We will have some answers soon enough. I'm headed back to the station. I'll see what dispatch has discovered."

Sarah was still crouched down and holding onto Whiskey because he wanted to play with Lilly. "Okay, Chief. Keep me posted."

As Chief James exited the Coiffure, Sarah let go of Whiskey and walked back to get started on Lilly. Her mind played over the events at the cafe in slow motion, like a football team meticulously reviewing game films of the opposing team. As if in a trance, she started Lilly's bath water and methodically prepared the grooming table as she had a thousand other times.

"Earth to Sarah. Earth to Sarah. We need to bust a move. We still have Charlie the Chinook for a spa treatment, Jazmin the little Yorkie for a simple grooming, and the new guy that came by last week with the black Newfoundland."

Snapping out of her trance, "Ben, his name is Ben and I believe the dog's name is Apollo. But I don't remember what Ben signed Apollo up for."

Emily stopped blow drying and brushing Spike for a few moments and shook out her arms and hands. "Why, why did we schedule three huge dogs in one day? Ugh, my arms and shoulders are already tired."

"I feel for you, Em, but we need to get through this long day."

Emily turned the blow dryer back on and resumed brushing Spike. "You ain't kidding. I'll be up late finishing school assignments, too."

As Emily was finishing Spike, Sarah started bathing Lilly, who looked like a majestic ship trying to squeeze into a tiny harbor. Her massive frame barely fit in the tub.

Emily placed the blow dryer back on the shelf and guided Spike off the table and onto the floor. She wasn't about to pick him up.

"Em, go ahead and text Tony and let him know we finished early with Spike."

Spike walked over to where Whiskey was now resting on the floor and sat next to him.

Emily said, "Wow. Spike looks like a perfectly chiseled sculpture."

"The statue of David was supposed to be the ideal of man. Spike is the ideal of man's best friend." Sarah smiled.

The remainder of the day went by quickly, but Sarah's mind wandered repeatedly back to the incident that morning at Java and Juice. She kept asking herself, what is Richard Clarkson's real story?

Sarah and Emily both worked the rest of the afternoon and into the evening. Tony returned for Spike, who wagged his tiny nub of a tail, clearly proud of his fresh look and happy to see his human. Holly and Lisa returned from their errands to find Lilly asleep on the floor in the corner with Whiskey. Charlie received an herbal shampoo and conditioner. Jazmin was scheduled for a simple grooming session, but since Emily was especially fond of the small and loveable canine, she pampered her with the new diluted tea tree line of products they were trying and gave her a blow out as well. The two master groomers finished the day by tag-teaming Apollo, the gentlest one hundred forty-pound dog in the world. With their teamwork and expertise, they managed to give the Newfoundland a thorough bath and blow dry in record time.

At six fifty p.m. Sarah and Emily finally turned off the lights to Carter's Canine Coiffure and stepped out onto the sidewalk with Whiskey by their sides. As Sarah closed and locked the forest green front door, she said, "What a day."

With a deep sigh and big stretch, extending her hands over her head, reaching toward the night sky, Emily said, "That's for sure. Do you realize that just with Spike, Lilly, and Apollo we washed over three hundred pounds of canine?"

"That was a lot of dogs, Em. I'm glad we don't have big dogs scheduled tomorrow."

Emily brought her hands and arms back down to her sides. "That's good." Emily walked across the street to her parked car. "See you in the morning, boss."

"Don't be up all-night texting Travis," Sarah joked.

Opening her driver's side car door, Emily snickered. "Oh, I won't, but I will be texting Travis."

Emily shut the car door, started the engine, and slowly pulled from the curb and continued down the street while Sarah and Whiskey walked down the sidewalk, taking their normal route home.

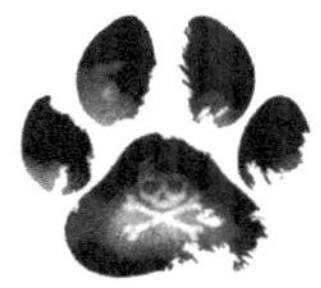

CHAPTER FIVE

At 7:07 a.m., Sarah and Whiskey strolled down Main Street, basking in the warmth of the morning sun's golden embrace, like a cozy blanket on a brisk morning. Whiskey was off leash and visiting every fire hydrant, sign post, and column along the sidewalk. He was Cottageville's socialite, greeting all the usual neighbors as he and his human made their daily trek to Carter's Canine Coiffure.

Sarah trailed after Whiskey, who was several paces ahead. She greeted the familiar faces with a forced smile. Her thoughts were consumed by yesterday's situation at Java and Juice. It was as if her mind was already inside her best friend's café, just a block away. She longed to have more information so that she could discuss it with Ginger and Jared. But all she knew was the name of the café's customer and that he had suffered a severe allergic reaction. The question that lingered in her mind was, *what was he allergic to?* It was like trying to start a five-thousand-piece puzzle without ever seeing the picture on the box.

Captivated by her thoughts, Sarah walked past Whiskey, who sat patiently outside Java and Juice's red door.

"Woof," Whiskey said, a staccato bark that got Sara's attention and forced her to do an about-face back to the entrance of Java and Juice. "You're so smart. You knew exactly where we were going," she said and scratched Whiskey's head with her right hand. As she pushed open the red door, she was reminded of her love for small-town living when she heard the familiar tinkle of the brass bell attached to the top of the doorframe.

The café was exceptionally quiet, although the regulars were seated at the tables enjoying their pastries and coffee. Many acknowledged Sarah and Whiskey's presence then went back to their conversations. Ginger and Jared were both busy preparing customers' orders and didn't notice Sarah enter. Sarah made her way to the display case, her attraction to the pastries was like a bee to jasmine, irresistibly drawn to the sweet temptations under the display lights. She smiled as she heard Jared frothing milk. There was something about the sound of frothing milk that made her heart happy, even though she never took her coffee with milk.

Whiskey parked himself next to the counter and waited while Sarah google-eyed the freshly made chocolate hazelnut puff pastry, classic cinnamon rolls, and one of her seasonal favorites, the German pumpkin streusel pastries. Ginger was getting a jumpstart on fall flavors though it was still summer.

Jared grabbed a small tin can off the counter and gently shook it over the Java and Juice coffee mug. The cinnamon and brown sugar mixture elevated the café's specialty drinks. Jared finished making the coffee and called out, "Ron, your coffee is up."

As he set Ron's cup on the counter under the overhanging 'pick-up here' sign, he noticed Sarah eyeing the pastries and looked as happy as a dog who had found a bone in a shrub. "Good morning, mi'lady."

"Morning, Jared. Um, sorry. Good morning, my lord."

Recognizing Sarah's lack of playfulness, Jared inquired, "What's up? What's on your mind?"

Before Sarah could respond, Whiskey gave a loud, "Wufffff," making it known he didn't like being ignored.

Reaching his hand over the counter, "Whiskey, my man, I didn't mean to ignore you. Give me some paw!"

Whiskey, familiar with all the terms, 'give me paw, give me dot, give me five,' sat back on his hind feet and threw his right paw against Jared's hand.

"That-a-boy!" Jared tossed Whiskey the café's homemade chicken bone-shaped dog treat.

"Now that I have taken care of Whiskey, what can I get for Ms. Carter?"

Sarah handed Jared her well-used 20-ounce reusable coffee tumbler, and said, "Give me four of the German pumpkin streusel pastries, please, my lord," As had become her signature move around Jared, she held her arms out as if clenching the sides of an imaginary skirt and curtsied.

Grinning, Jared said, "Wow, four streusel pastries. I promise I won't tell anyone."

Sarah joked, "Don't worry, I'll devour all four of them and dispose of the bag before I even reach my shop. That way there won't be any proof. It'll just be a case of your word against mine."

"But I will have a copy of your credit card receipt in the register," Jared said.

"Well then I guess I am paying with cash today. And no tip for you either, since you are trying to blackmail me."

Jared and Sarah both laughed, and Sarah felt her mood lighten.

Jared turned toward the coffee machine and filled Sarah's cup and then screwed its lid tight. He retrieved the pastries from the display case and placed them in a brown paper bag with the Java and Juice logo stamped on the outside. He handed Sarah her oversized tumbler and the brown paper bag. "Anything else?"

With her mind now off yesterday morning's happenings and feeling a little giddy, Sarah said, "Why yes, my lord, there is something else. You asked me out on a date for this week, but still haven't told me when. And since today is Friday and the week is almost over..." Her voice trailed off.

Cutting in, like a child secretly eavesdropping on her parent's private conversation, Ginger asked, "Did I hear the word date?"

Jared turned the color of a merlot. "Umm, maybe."

With a smile extending from cheek to cheek, Ginger said, "Forgive my intrusion then," and chuckled.

Sarah admired her best friend's smile and clear complexion. "I don't know, Ginger. Jared said he wanted to take me out, but right now I think he's all talk."

Jared cleared his throat before saying, "You are right, mi'lady. I have not technically asked you out. So, what about tonight?"

Ginger walked two feet away and focused again on a customer's order.

"I can't tonight. I am taking Gladys Rossmiller to look at poodles after I get off work."

Jared pursed his lips. "Tomorrow then?"

"Tomorrow it is."

"It will be fun. I already have something planned, but I want it to be a surprise."

Smiling and reaching into her jeans pocket for her credit card, Sarah admitted, "I am looking forward to it."

Sarah tapped her credit card on the screen and left her usual twenty-percent tip.

With a sparkle in his eyes, Jared pointed his finger at the iPad, "I now have the evidence. Sarah Carter ordered and ate four German pumpkin streusel pastries!"

"Very funny, wise guy. You keep it up and you will be going on a date by yourself!"

Jared overlapped his hands on his chest. "Ouch, mi'lady just ran me through."

Sarah grinned and turned around. "Come on, Whiskey, let's get out of this place before I really do run Jared through."

As Sarah and Whiskey were walking toward the door to exit Java and Juice, she quickly turned and ran back to where Ginger was behind the counter. Setting her tumbler and brown paper bag on the counter, Sarah reached over the counter and wrapped her arms around Ginger's shoulders and neck. "I love you, bestie. You need to come over soon and enjoy a bottle of syrah with me."

"I'd love to; it's been a hot minute."

Letting go of Ginger's neck, Sarah said, "Text me later. Love you."

"Love you too, girl."

"All right, Whiskey, we are actually leaving this time."

With his barrel chest and head held high, Whiskey resembled a gallant knight leading his human out of the café.

Sarah couldn't wait to arrive at her shop and share the seasonal pumpkin streusel pastries with Emily. Whiskey got there first and faced the green front door, waiting patiently for Sarah to catch up and push the door open. Emily was already busy inside, with the door unlocked, lights on, and her favorite EMO playlist blaring through the shop.

Pushing the door open, Sarah said, "Good morning, Em."

Still cleaning the front counter with unscented, biodegradable wipes, Emily looked up. "Morning, boss." She changed the tone of her voice to ooze enthusiasm when she addressed Whiskey. "Good morning, handsome boy."

Raising up the brown paper bag with the Java and Juice logo, Sarah said, "Guess what I got us?"

"A bag of cash. I told you not to rob the First Colonial Bank."

Giggling, Sarah said, "If I robbed the local bank, I better walk away with more than a small paper bag."

"True, but this is a small town."

"Good point. It's not money, but it is Java and Juice's decadent

German pumpkin streusel pastries."

"Yes!" Emily pumped her fist near her chest. "I love those."

Setting the bag and her tumbler on the just cleaned counter, Sarah pulled the appointment book off the shelf and began to look over the day.

"I glanced over our schedule and all our clients are under twenty pounds, so it's going to be a busy but easy day."

"Awesome. Let's enjoy our pastries before Tiny the toy poodle arrives."

Tearing off two paper towels from the roll, Emily handed one to Sarah and placed the other one on the counter for herself. Sarah reached into the paper bag and placed two pastries on Emily's paper towel and two on her own. Emily picked up a glass jar under the counter and pulled out an organic cowhide chew and tossed it to Whiskey. Whiskey lunged forward and caught it in his mouth, then laid down by the front door to enjoy his treat.

In between bites of her pastry, Emily asked, "Any news on the guy at Java and Juice yesterday?"

"I haven't heard anything, but I sure hope we find out something soon."

"Was the guy alone yesterday morning?"

"That's a good question. I would assume so since no one responded to him when he slammed his fist on the table."

"Why don't you call Jared or Ginger and ask them to pull the video footage from yesterday morning?"

"Listen to you, Nancy Drew."

Emily grinned. "Very funny, it was just an idea."

"It's a great idea. I'll call them now."

Sarah reached into the back right pocket of her blue jeans and pulled out her cell phone. Speaking into her phone, she said, "Siri, call Jared."

After two rings, Jared answered, "Sarah."

Sarah launched in without greeting him, "Do you think Ginger's cameras recorded Mr. Clarkson entering Java and Juice yesterday?"

"What? Who?"

Recognizing her lack of clarity, she said, "I'm sorry, Jared. Richard Clarkson is the guy who had the allergic reaction yesterday morning. I was wondering if he was alone. That's why I wanted to know if the cameras might have recorded him entering the café."

"Come on, Sherlock Holmes. You are one step behind. Officer Beams called Ginger right after you left and asked her to pull the footage, so she is presently going over it."

"Oh wow. Jared, do you remember if Richard Clarkson was with anyone?"

"Sarah, I honestly can't remember. I know I served him and didn't recognize him, but other than that, I've got nothing."

"Okay."

"So, what exactly should Ginger be looking for in the video footage?"

"To see if Mr. Clarkson was with someone."

Jared laughed into the phone. "You love this detective stuff, don't you?"

"You know I do." Just then Sarah received an incoming call from John Beams. "Jared, I gotta go. Officer Beams is calling."

Disconnecting with Jared and swiping to answer, Sarah heard the officer say, "Good morning, Sarah. Dispatch found the call in the log and ran the number. The call was placed approximately fifteen minutes before you yelled for someone to call nine-one-one and the number is Richard's. I just hung up with the chief, who will be headed to the hospital later this morning to talk to Mr. Clarkson."

"No way! If Richard called nine-one-one, that means he knew he was going to have an allergic reaction and that he would need help," exclaimed Sarah.

"It sounds like a possibility, but it's too early, and could be counterproductive, to draw any conclusions. We should know more once the chief gets to the hospital."

"This is crazy. What are the chances of us having another mysterious happening right here in Cottageville so soon?"

With skepticism in his voice, Officer Beams said, "I'm not sure what's going on, but are you ready to be a detective again?"

Sarah giggled. "I'm not sure I have completely recovered from what happened with Mrs. Jenkins. Yet, on the other hand, I am ready to take on another case."

"I think the appropriate question is, is Whiskey ready?"

Laughing, Sarah said, "Good point. He is in the zone this morning, going to town on a cowhide chew, but I bet he'd love to solve another mystery. Right, Whiskey?"

At the mention of his name, Whiskey stopped chewing for a moment, kept his head in the same position, resting on his paws extended in front of him, but he lifted his gaze toward Sarah.

"He's alert and ready," she said into the phone.

"I'll let you know when we find something out, Sarah. Have a good day."

"Thanks. You, too."

Sarah placed her phone on the counter and told Emily about Richard calling nine-one-one himself. As they finished their last bites of the sweet and spicy pumpkin strudel pastries, Tiny the toy poodle arrived in the arms of his human, Rosa Torres. Rosa had olive skin, dark black hair, and resembled a princess from a Disney movie. She appeared to be in her twenties but was in her forties.

"Good morning, ladies. I hope I am not interrupting your breakfast," said Rosa as she entered the Coiffure and walked toward the counter.

"Not at all, Mrs. Torres." Emily said, wiping her mouth with a paper towel before balling it in her fist and throwing it away.

Rosa set Tiny on the counter. She shivered as her black eyes stared up at Emily.

"Here you go, girl," Emily said, scooping the dog against her apron. "I've got you."

"I'll be back in two hours," Rosa said, before heading out the door.

CHAPTER SIX

The day went by fast as Emily and Sarah expressed anal glands, clipped nails and dewclaws, brushed teeth, and washed and dried small dog after dog. At exactly five forty-five, Whiskey stood at attention and barked once as Gladys pulled up in front of Carter's Canine Coiffure. Sarah said goodnight to Emily, who was clipping the nails of one last dog. Emily promised to lock up when she was done and after Cheech the chihuahua had been picked up.

Sarah opened the back door of the silver Camry and told Whiskey to get in, and then she entered the shotgun seat. Gladys wore a pastel blue sweater over her flowered blouse to protect against the evening breeze. "Thank you for going with me, Sarah," she said as

Sarah buckled her seat belt. "And you too, Whiskey." Gladys reached over the seat, and Whiskey slurped her hand with his tongue. She laughed and then put the car in drive.

Classical music played softly in the background as they headed north out of downtown Cottageville. "Their website shows six poodles, two standard size and two minis and two teacups," Gladys explained as she drove. "But I called earlier today, and they said they had three puppies, as one of the minis was pregnant when it was rescued. I'm not sure I want the work of housebreaking." Gladys frowned. "Oh and someone dropped off two new dogs yesterday."

"Training is a lot of responsibility and time," Sarah agreed. "Did they say if the others were trained already?"

"I believe so."

"Do you know the ages of the others?" Sarah reasoned that a young dog, especially a standard, which could weigh as much as seventy pounds, would be too much for Gladys to handle. She wanted her friend to adopt a middle-aged mini or teacup, something that wouldn't likely pull her over and wouldn't have high-strung puppy energy or too much prey instinct. Over the millennia, poodles had been bred for hunting and had been known to go after squirrels, cats, ducks, geese, rabbits, and an occasional large animal like a bear. Sarah could envision Gladys being pulled into someone's yard if the poodle lunged for a bird. She didn't want to see her face plant or break a hip.

"I don't remember," Gladys said. "I'm sure they can tell us when we get there."

"You let them know that Whiskey was joining us, right?"

Gladys grinned. "Of course, dear. He's a member of our tribe, as I believe you young people say."

"He is. Thank you." Sarah looked over her left shoulder to see Whiskey sitting upright with his back end on the seat like a human, looking out the window. He was smiling.

In fewer than eight minutes, Gladys turned into a semi-paved driveway that ran through fields of rye, though Sarah could see a field of corn stalks starting to dry and brown in the distance. The driveway ended at a white two-story farmhouse with navy blue shutters and a big wraparound porch complete with seven wooden rocking chairs, each painted one color of the rainbow and in order from left to right: red, orange, yellow, green, blue, indigo, and violet. The screen door opened and slapped shut as they parked, and before Gladys had shut off the engine, the Camry was surrounded by the frenetic energy of a dozen poodles in a range of grays, apricot, reds, whites, and cafe au lait. Some of the dogs were tall enough to look into the car windows, while the tops of others' heads didn't even clear the Camry's tires.

Whiskey hit the back passenger side window twice with his paw, demanding to be let out to romp with the pack.

"Hey, let them get out of the car," said a fair skinned woman in her late thirties in worn jeans and a heather gray "Anatomy of a Poodle" t-shirt. Her pale hair was in a single braid down her back.

A bald man wearing a trucker's hat, a weathered denim shirt, tan work pants, and muck boots parted the dogs at Gladys' door and reached for the handle. Sarah pegged him to be in his early forties. "You must be Gladys," he said, opening her door. He held out his calloused hand to help her from the car. "I'm so sorry for your loss."

Gladys' eyes filled but didn't overflow as she took his hand and accepted his help. "Thank you. You're very kind."

Sarah eased her door open so she wouldn't bang it into a dog, and as she started to get out of the car, Whiskey jumped over the seat and pushed past her. "Dog," Sarah muttered, chuckling and reprimanding at the same time. "You only saved yourself a second, two tops."

But Whiskey didn't hear her as he was running flat out and leading the pack in circles as they chased him. His tongue hung from the side of his jaw. He was having the time of his life.

Sarah walked behind the car to where Gladys, the man, and now the woman were standing.

Gladys said, "Donovan, this is my friend Sarah. She owns Carter's Canine Coiffure and knows more about dogs than anyone I know, other than maybe Dr. Schank, my vet."

Sarah held out her hand. "Pleased to meet you," she said as they shook.

"This is my wife Daisy," Donovan said. Sarah smiled at the woman before shaking her hand.

Gladys leaned toward Daisy while saying, "I'm more of a hugger myself, if you don't mind."

Daisy chuckled. "Of course not," she said and embraced Gladys.

"That's Whiskey running around with your pack," Sarah said. "Thank you for letting him come along."

"Of course," Donovan said. "There are few breeds that can keep up with poodles, but your working dog is doing a fine job."

The dogs were running through the fields now with the biggest dogs in the lead and Whiskey close on their heels. The smaller sized poodles tried to keep up but their shorter legs weren't built for long-distance speed. A silver mini and an apricot teacup returned to the humans within minutes.

"This is Fred," Donovan said, bending to work his fingers in the tight curls on the silver dog's head. Fred leaned into Donovan's hand encouraging him to massage his head even more.

"And this is Princess," Daisy said, scooping up the teacup poodle and holding the dog close to her chest. "Both are available for adoption. But let's also go inside so you can see the latest litter and meet the dogs who don't get free reign of the property. These ones are the newest rescues."

Daisy led the way through the screen door, and Donovan held the door for Gladys and Sarah. Before Sarah entered she looked around for Whiskey but couldn't see him, only movement through the corn stalks.

"Don't worry," Donovan said. "They won't let him leave the grounds."

Sarah smiled and nodded her head. "I wasn't as worried about him as I was that he'd be worried about me if I couldn't see me," she admitted.

"We have a big dog door in the back. He'll come in with the others, I'm sure."

"Okay," Sarah said. She followed the sound of Gladys and Daisy's voices into the kitchen, which had a white and red gingham ruffle valance atop a big picture window over a white enameled sink. The counters were spotless except for more than a dozen stainless steel bowls lined up in anticipation of the dogs' next meal. A stainless steel watering trough with an inverted three gallon water jug sat in one corner of an open area where a kitchen table may have once lived. Next to that water jug was a metal wire fenced-off area where, on a mound of old towels, a mama poodle lay on her side while three squirming, sucking puppies fed. One puppy was red, one was black, and one was black with a blob of white on its forehead. Their eyes were closed.

"How old are they?" Sarah asked.

"Six days," Daisy said. "There was a fourth one, but it didn't make it."

"Such as shame," Gladys said.

"The puppies will be ready in about seven more weeks," Donovan said.

"They are cute," Gladys said, eyeing them. "Especially that black and white one. But I think my puppy care days are behind me. You said you have others?"

"Yes," Daisy said. She led the way through the house and out the back door and into a barn that smelled of hay and horses though none were in sight. She stopped at the first stall and looked over the door. Sarah and Gladys did the same. Two miniature poodles were curled into a ball together on an old blanket. They were sound asleep.

"You have visitors," Daisy said as she tapped on their barn door. The chocolate colored poodle jumped and barked as it raced to the door.

"She's a feisty one." Gladys smiled.

"She is," Donovan said. "Someone saw her on the side of the interstate and brought her to us yesterday. She was not chipped and didn't have a collar. She saw the vet this morning and got some shots. She's scheduled to get fixed next week."

"And the other one?" Sarah asked.

"Was with this one. She was frightened of our friend who stopped and cowered while the other postured like she'd rip his arm off."

"I hope he was unhurt," Gladys said, eying the little dog who stood on its hind legs like a dog in a circus. All it was missing was the tutu.

"He's fine. He's dealt with afraid strays before. He's a bit of a dog and horse whisperer. He was able to get them both in his truck and calm them before he brought them to us."

The chocolate dog sat on its haunches by the door and wagged its tail while the blue poodle eyed them suspiciously from a safe distance.

As Daisy moved to open the door to the stall, Sarah heard the pounding of feet behind her. She turned her head toward the barn door and saw Whiskey and his new friends race into the barn. He stopped short next to her and slurped her fingers with his tongue. "You having fun, boy?"

Whiskey grinned up at her.

Daisy and Donovan both laughed. Then Daisy pushed the stall door open and slid inside. "You want to meet them?" she asked Gladys and Sarah.

Before Gladys answered, Whiskey pushed inside the stall and curled himself into a ball on the floor. The poodles—one confident and in command and one shyly—approached him and sniffed him all over. He was still and waited until they were through.

The shy one sat down against him, like she had known him all of her life.

The chocolate dog, instead, walked to Gladys and sat on her foot. Her black eyes implored Gladys to pick her up.

"Ha ha," Daisy said. "It looks like you've been chosen."

Sarah bent and picked up the chocolate dog and handed her to Gladys since she figured her almost-octogenarian friend might need some assistance.

As soon as the dog was in Gladys' arms, it snuggled its head under her chin. "That tickles," Gladys said, her knobby fingers caressing the springy poodle fur. To Daisy and Donovan she said, "I don't know. I wasn't planning on two dogs. Only one. But it seems a shame to separate them. They seem as close as Van Gogh and Gauguin."

"You don't have to feel pressured to get both," Donovan said. "We almost always find homes for them."

"Are they housebroken?" Sarah asked.

"We think," Daisy admitted, "but we aren't certain. Like we said, we got them yesterday and took them for part of their shots this morning. We were keeping them separate from the others until they were up to date on the shots. They both will be spayed on Monday. We think they have been trained because they seem to hate going to the bathroom in this stall. I've been taking them out every couple of hours into the grass and they seem to know exactly what to do and have clearly been on leashes before."

All human eyes looked from one dog to the other. The dog curled with Whiskey had fallen asleep and was snoring, sounding like a buzzing bee. The dog in Gladys' arms let out a sigh. Sarah sensed these dogs really had chosen them. But she didn't want a poodle. She wondered if she and Gladys could talk Bill into taking one of them, if Gladys decided two was too much.

"Did the vet say how old he or she thought the dogs were?" Gladys asked.

"Older than two but not yet seniors. It's difficult to age a dog properly unless they have a lot of wear on their teeth or still have their puppy teeth," Daisy explained.

The dog in Gladys' arms sighed again.

Sarah smiled. "I think that dog wants to go home with you right now and that Whiskey has found himself a VELCRO® dog."

They all looked down at Whiskey who appeared as happy as a person who won a million bucks on a scratch-off lottery ticket.

"So if they are having surgery on Monday, when will they be ready to be moved to a new home?" Gladys asked.

Donovan said, "Dogs start feeling better in forty-eight hours, but it is usually about two weeks until they are released from their activity restrictions."

"Hmm," Gladys said aloud. "Life seems pretty active here. My house might be quieter for recovery."

Daisy smiled. "I'm sure that is true. But we cannot in good conscience adopt out a dog or dogs who haven't been fixed yet. If you want a dog sooner than two weeks, maybe we should look at the others we have available."

Gladys hugged the dog she was holding and then pressed her lips to the top of its head.

Sarah knew this was a sign that Gladys would wait for that dog.

"I don't want to see the others," Gladys said. She looked down at the dog in her arms. "What do you think of the name Kahlo? You seem bold like Frida."

Sarah chuckled. "Maybe Janice or Bill will take Kahlo's friend or sibling."

Gladys looked from Sarah to the dog with Whiskey. "No, I do believe Cassatt will also be coming home with me. Two small dogs can't be much more trouble than one. Especially at this size." She hefted the ten pound dog away from her chest. "Not much more than a sack of flour."

Sarah, Daisy, and Donovan laughed, and then Donovan said, "I'm sure they will love living with you."

"So it's settled then," Gladys said. She kissed Kahlo on the head again. "Take care, spirited girl. I'll come get you in two weeks." To Donovan and Daisy she said, "Would it be okay if I came back a couple of times next week to visit? I don't want them to think I've forgotten them."

"Of course," Daisy said. "Just text us or call us that you are coming. You're welcome any time."

"Thank you." Gladys handed the dog to Daisy. "Would you like a deposit?"

Daisy put the dog on the floor of the stall and it curled up with a sigh.

Donovan and Gladys walked a few feet to a workbench and went over the details of the deposit, and Gladys signed the adoption papers.

Daisy said to Sarah, "That's one sweet cattle dog you have."

Whiskey picked up his head and smiled at them. "Yes, and he's a character, too," Sarah said.

"Aren't they all?" Two standard poodles ran into the barn. One had a squirrel in its mouth. "Not again," Daisy said when she saw it. "Drop it."

The rust colored poodle opened its jaws and deposited its catch at her feet. It looked up at her for praise. "Good boy," she said, patting its head as it thumped its tail.

To Sarah, she said, "I know it's his instincts, but sometimes I root for the squirrel." Daisy grabbed a shovel and scooped the dead rodent from the barn floor and put it in a black plastic bag lined garbage can.

Sarah called for Whiskey to say goodbye to his new friends, and after he exited the stall, Daisy shut its door. Gladys said her goodbyes and made promises to "her girls" over the door, before they all walked around the house to the driveway. Gladys hugged her goodbyes to Daisy and Donovan as Sarah secured Whiskey into the back of the car.

When she slid behind the wheel of her Camry, Gladys' face was beaming. "I'm so tickled. Who knew I'd find two dogs instead of one. Thank you, Sarah, for accompanying me."

"You're welcome. But if two ends up being too much, I'll help you talk Janice or Bill into taking one of them."

"You're a dear," Gladys said, patting Sarah's hand. "But I'm committed to doing this. Kahlo and Cassatt need me." She grinned at Sarah and then started the car.

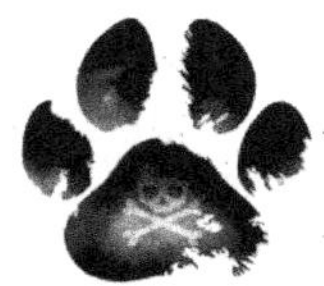

CHAPTER SEVEN

Sarah awoke as the sun was rising Saturday morning because thirty-five pounds of cattle dog sat atop her chest. When she opened her eyes, Whiskey licked the tip of her nose. Then he jumped from the bed, barked once that translated to a "human, follow me" command, and ran from the room.

"Hold on, hold on," Sarah said, padding in bare feet to the bathroom and grabbing the white Turkish cotton robe hanging from the back of the door.

Whiskey was impatiently waiting by the back door. His eyes were huge, and he pawed the door as if telling her, "Come on, come on. I don't want to have an accident, but I'm about to detonate."

Sarah speedwalked the rest of the way to the door, unlocked it, and pushed it open. Whiskey took a flying leap through the doorway and off the back cement stoop onto the grass below. He squatted immediately and smiled at her like peeing was the best thing ever.

"I get it," Sarah said, since she needed to do the same. She left the back door agape and took care of her own business before heading to the kitchen to pour Whiskey a cup of his grain-free kibble. She ground dark roast beans before dumping them into the reusable filter and then added water to the coffee maker and turned it on.

As the coffee maker did its thing, she wondered what was taking Whiskey so long. Sarah belted her robe tighter around her waist as she stuck her head out the back door. She looked left and then right before spying Whiskey's fluffy white-tipped tail poking from around the side of the house. "What the heck—" she mumbled, before stepping barefoot on the grass and walking his way.

Whiskey sat at attention below a fence post, his tail thumping on the ground and his head cocked sideways. Robert Wise's orange and white striped cat sat atop the post licking one of its front paws and then the other. It oozed nonchalance, but Sarah knew that the cat knew its presence and actions were driving Whiskey crazy.

He whined when Sarah approached. "I know, boy. You'd love to play with Mozart, but just like the squirrels, he only wants to mess with you, make you beg for it, and watch you cry. Let's go inside. I have your breakfast ready."

At the word breakfast, Whiskey's ears twitched his happiness, and he took off toward the house. Sarah bid a good day to Mozart and followed her dog. She heard his metal tags banging against his bowl as she closed and locked the back door.

Sarah took her freshly poured mug of black coffee back to her bedroom. She propped up some pillows before sitting back against them with her down-filled white duvet over her legs. Then she picked up her phone, turned off its sleep mode, and switched the ringer back on. A text popped up from Jared: "Wear jeans, tennis shoes, and layers for tonight's date. I'll swing by at 5. Whiskey is welcome to come, too."

"Oh so we are going somewhere fancy," Sarah replied, hoping he could hear the teasing tone of her text.

"Only the best for mi'lady."

Sarah smiled.

"Or for mi'lady and her non-mutt," Jared added.

Sarah laughed aloud.

"I'll pack his supper to go."

"No need," Jared said. "I have it taken care of."

Hmm, Sarah thought. She loved that Jared understood she and Whiskey were a package deal, but she was a bit disappointed not to have the night off or to have Jared to herself on their first date. She wondered what he had planned.

"I can get him a sitter," she texted. "Or, he is old enough to be home by himself for a few hours."

"Absolutely not," Jared replied. "Whiskey would never forgive me."

Sarah smiled again. "Especially if there is food."

"Right. Until this afternoon." Jared ended the text conversation.

Sarah sipped more coffee and stretched just as Whiskey entered the bedroom. "Do you need to go out again?" she asked. "Or if you can wait ten minutes, I'll shower and then we can walk. How's that sound?"

In response, Whiskey jumped onto the bed, circled once to collect the duvet into a mound, and curled himself into a ball atop it and closed his eyes.

"The shower it is then," Sarah muttered as she walked into the bathroom carrying her cup of coffee.

Twenty minutes later, Sarah's to-go coffee tumbler was in her hand, and she was on the sidewalk in front of Bill's house while Whiskey sat next to Bill on his porch and chomped on a biscuit.

"How did it go at the poodle pound?" Bill asked, the skin around his eyes wrinkling in laughter.

"Have you talked to her?" Sarah asked, setting her tumbler on the sidewalk. She pulled her University of Washington Husky sweatshirt over her head and tied it around her waist. The day was hotter than she was expecting at this hour.

"I did. She said she found a new dog but wanted it to be a surprise and wouldn't say anything more."

"Okay," Sarah said, glad she asked a question instead of answering Bill's. "Well then you're getting nothing from me other than they had a whole pack of poodles. So many. And the couple seemed super sweet. They said they have been rescuing dogs for almost two decades."

"That's a long time," Bill said. "You want to come up and sit down?"

"No, thank you. Whiskey and I need to be on our way. Whiskey, stop begging for another treat. Come down here."

Whiskey rolled his eyes toward Bill and then back at Sarah. He hung his head and slunk down the stairs.

"Thank you for the treat, Bill. We appreciate it."

"Any time." Bill returned to the newspaper in front of him.

Sarah and Whiskey started past Java and Juice since she already had her coffee, but she made a mental note that the place was packed. She could see Barbara Order, the chief's brassy blonde wife, holding court with her three closest friends. They were all in Spandex like they had come from the yoga studio. Barbara was facing the window and waved to Sarah to enter the cafe so she pushed its red door and held it open for Whiskey, who beelined for the counter and the treat jar.

"Sarah," Barbara exclaimed. "Have you heard?"

Sarah strolled to the table and greeted each woman by name before saying, "Heard what?"

"That man, the one who was here and choking or whatever, he was gone when James returned to the hospital to ask about his call to nine-one-one. The hospital staff said he didn't even discharge himself. He just left. Not a word to anyone."

"What? Seriously?" Sarah's brow furrowed. "That's crazy and highly suspicious."

"I know, right?!" Barbara said. "No reason to run unless you're doing something wrong."

"Is there an APB out on him?" Sarah asked as she saw Ginger hand a homemade dog treat to Whiskey. "Only one," she yelled to her BFF. "He's already visited Bill this morning."

"Okay. No more," Ginger said. She held up her hands in surrender. Her golden curls were piled atop her head in a messy bun.

Her Java and Juice apron covered her hot pink t-shirt and jeans.

"No APB. James said they still don't know if he broke any laws. I mean it isn't against the law to call emergency services before you need them."

"But it is super weird," Barbara's best friend and Cottageville's mayor Trish McGowan said.

"Yes, but if James had to arrest everyone who did something weird, this town would be empty," Barbara said, before throwing her head back in a cackle like she had amused herself.

"True," Trish admitted. "Or at least most of it."

"Yes, even you did weird things here in Cottageville as a teen," Barbara reminded her. "Back when your dad was the mayor."

"Don't remind me," Trish said and then laughed. "Some of those weird things were with you, Babs."

Sarah thought that was the one disadvantage of staying where you grew up: everyone knew everything about you, your history, your good and bad choices, your life. "Thanks for letting me know, Barbara. I appreciate it. Come on, Whiskey."

Sarah left Java and Juice and instead of walking, she jogged. Despite his shorter legs, Whiskey kept pace and a few blocks in, he looked up at her and winked. "We've gotta get home," Sarah huffed, slightly winded as they ran through the park. "I have an idea."

As they jogged down their street, Sarah mumbled a mantra of "Richard Clarkson, Richard Clarkson. Who are you, Richard Clarkson? I'm coming to find you, Richard Clarkson."

When her keys were in her front door and she pushed it open, Sarah said aloud, "Ready or not, here I come."

She grabbed her laptop from the counter and sat on her sofa cross legged with the computer on her lap. She typed in her password and then opened her browser. She spelled out Richard Clarkson and put his name in quotation marks and then clicked search.

The first five hits on the man's name weren't social media like Sarah would have expected. They were links to lawsuits in Portland, Oregon; Tallahassee, Florida; Kansas City, Missouri; Grand Forks, North Dakota; and Tulsa, Oklahoma. R. Clarkson v. *[insert name of local restaurant]*.

Sarah started shaking. *Oh my, Richard, you really are a dick,* she thought. She reached for her phone but wasn't sure who to call first, Ginger to tell her about the bullet she dodged, Officer Beams to check if they had done a simple web search, or the chief to say that Richard Clarkson has been scheming all over. Then reason took over and she told Siri to call John Beams. Police first. Then she and Ginger could gossip once Ginger closed the cafe for the day.

As she waited for John to pick up, Sarah opened the first lawsuit and started to read. When he didn't answer, Sarah left a message. "Officer Beams, it's Sarah, though I'm sure you know that from the caller I.D. Anyway, I Googled Richard Clarkson and it turns out he's filed a lot of lawsuits against restaurants all over the country for making him sick and making him suffer. If you haven't looked him up, I think you should. You don't need to call me back. Have a happy Saturday."

Then she texted Ginger: "Call me when you're done for the day. Thanks."

Sarah set her laptop aside and went into the kitchen and made herself another cup of coffee and scrambled an egg, which she ate atop sourdough toast. Then she dove back into the deep ocean of the world wide web, jotting notes on a legal pad, looking for any and every mention of Richard Clarkson she could find. Whiskey provided moral support by curling onto the sofa next to her and taking a nap.

The lawsuits where R. Clarkson was the defendant went back years. Sarah opened a Word doc and created a timeline, with hyperlinks to each court's recording of the suit. She added notes on the judgments against most of the cafes and restaurants.

The more she read, the more anger burbled like a volcano inside her. What Dick—she refused to call him Richard anymore—Clarkson did was out and out fraud. How was he getting away with it?

Sarah felt certain that he would try to serve Ginger with a lawsuit. She couldn't let that happen.

Sarah spent another two hours collecting all of the information she could on the schemer, including creating a list of his previously known addresses. At one point, she stumbled across a barely followed Instagram account that he started a few years before where he checked in at cafes and coffee houses and posted pictures of what he ordered. Sarah cross referenced those couple of dozen postings with the list of places he had sued. Three-quarters of them he had filed judgments against for food poisoning or undisclosed allergens and causing him mental distress and bodily harm.

She added a screenshot of his Instagram account to her Word document, and once she felt like she had enough ammunition, she called Chief James.

He answered on the first ring. "Hello, Sarah."

"Hi, Chief. I want to send you over a file I compiled today. I did a lot of online research on Richard Clarkson. Not sure if you or your officers have searched the web, but he's left quite a trail of lawsuits in his wake. All against restaurants, cafes, and coffee shops, both mom and pop places and a few national chains for basically the same type of event, if you will, that happened at Java and Juice."

"Wow, Sarah. That's great detective work. We hadn't looked for lawsuits, since as far as we knew he hadn't committed a crime."

"I think he's defrauded people out of a lot of money. Maybe millions. I'd like to send you over what I put together so you can see if there's any legal recourse."

"I'm happy to take a look. But unless he sues Ginger or the Parks' ambulance service or the hospital, I'm not sure what we can do."

Sarah audibly sighed. "I can't stand when people get away with stuff like this. It isn't right."

"I agree with you. Send over what you've put together and maybe I'll make some calls and see what we can come up with. Thank you for your work on this, Sarah. You're a good friend to everyone in this town."

"Thank you, Chief. The document is on its way. Enjoy the rest of your Saturday."

"You, too," Chief James said.

Sarah disconnected and felt despair like a lead balloon in her gut. She didn't want Java and Juice or any company to be helpless and victimized by a shyster like Dick Clarkson. There had to be something they could do, even if the police could do nothing.

Sarah planned to ask Jared to help her brainstorm during their date. She was sure they could come up with a solution. They made a great investigative team.

Neither Ginger nor Officer Beams returned Sarah's messages.

But a few hours later Whiskey raced from the back of the house to the front door, almost sliding into it on the hardwoods when the doorbell rang. He barked twice and stood on his hind legs to look out the window. He cocked his head sideways when he saw Jared. Whiskey smiled showing his black gums and white teeth.

"Move back, dog," Sarah said as she opened the door. She wore her favorite pair of jeans with a forest green "I kissed a dog and I liked it" t-shirt and a flannel shirt tied around her waist for later. Her carrot-y colored hair was down around her face in soft waves, and she had swiped her lashes with mascara and painted her lips red for the date.

Jared had a backpack slung over one shoulder. "Mi'lady, you look beautiful tonight."

"As do you, my lord." And he did. Sarah noted that blue-green, the color of the Caribbean Sea, really complemented his complexion and eyes.

"Are we ready to go?"

"I think so," Sarah said.

"Are you ready, Whiskey?" Jared asked.

Whiskey mouthed Jared's jeans near the ankle in response. Jared laughed. "And that's why you are a heeler. Come on." He motioned for them to walk across the street.

Sarah pulled the door shut on her house and locked it. Then she caught up to Jared and Whiskey who was walking by his side. They strolled down the street to its dead end and then Jared started into the woods. It was the first time they had come this way since they searched for Janice Jenkins when she went missing.

"How was your day?" Jared asked as they meandered down the dirt path that swerved through the oaks, maples, and hickory trees.

Whiskey ran out ahead of them by at least a yard and followed all of the scents in the forest, zigzagging back and forth across the path.

"I spent a lot of the day researching that guy who had the allergic reaction in your cafe, and I found out he's quite the con man. He's sued so many restaurants all around the country for, I'm guessing, the exact same shenanigans he pulled at Java and Juice. And what's worse is that he's won."

"No way!" Jared said. "That's awful."

"Yep. But Chief James said so far they cannot tie him to a crime in Cottageville."

"Well that sucks. He needs to be stopped."

"Exactly. Which is why I figured we could brainstorm what we can do. I even found an old IG account of his where he posted photos of some of the food and drinks he ordered from places before he sued them."

Jared narrowed his eyes and frowned. "When he sued them, did you see on what grounds?"

"Claimed food poisoning or undisclosed allergens, depending where or when. Always sought medical attention so he had official proof and claimed mental and emotional distress, time lost from work..." Sarah's voice trailed off before she added, "It makes me so mad. You know it was all a bunch of crap. I mean you saw what happened. And why would he throw away a perfectly good orange? That makes no sense."

They came to the end of the path and the woods and before them was a lush field of wildflowers. Bees and hummingbirds buzzed around them as they followed a trail cut through the flowers and tall grasses. Whiskey led the way as if he knew where they were going, but Jared still hadn't said.

"Wait." Jared suddenly stopped and turned his head to face Sarah. "Did Beams or the Parks find a needle?"

"They didn't mention one. Why?"

"Well, what if the dude bought the orange because he had a needle filled with whatever he's allergic to, but he knew he could only inject part of the syringe into himself—"

Sarah cut him off, "Because he'd OD with the whole thing?" Joy bubbled within her. That seemed brilliant as well as sneaky scary. "So you're saying that they need to test that orange for some kind of allergen, that he injected the orange with half or a part of the allergen. Oh my! You're an evil genius." Sarah hugged him.

The sound of Jared's hearty laughter reverberated against her heart.

Sarah stepped back. "Um, sorry. I didn't mean to force a hug on you."

Jared grinned. "There was no forcing. I welcomed it. I'll welcome it again, in fact."

Sarah smiled. "Well okay then." She embraced him and let him go quickly. "So we need to tell that idea to the chief. I'm going to text him now." She pulled her phone from her back pocket and wrote a fast recap of the idea and asked if the lab could check for known anaphylactic-inducing allergies in the orange.

Then Jared led her to just before the old water tower in the field. "We are stopping here." He pulled the backpack off his shoulder and pulled out a blanket. Sarah helped him open it and stretch it onto the grass. Whiskey made it his own immediately by curling up on one corner of it.

Jared set a metal bowl next to Whiskey and filled it with water. He opened the lid on a smaller metal bowl and said to Sarah, "Chopped chicken and sweet potatoes. Is it okay if I give it to him?"

"Absolutely." She was touched by his thoughtfulness. "Did you make that for him?"

"Yes. I cooked the breast and the potato in some broth so it wouldn't dry out for him."

"He's a spoiled beast," Sarah said.

"But we wouldn't have it any other way," Jared said, looking down at Whiskey as he gobbled the food like he hadn't eaten all day.

Jared pulled a bottle of champagne from the backpack, along with two glasses, two melamine plates, blue checked cloth napkins, and metal silverware. He had prepared a bowl of curried chicken salad with chopped celery and dried currants, a homemade coleslaw with grated carrots and a pinch of paprika, and two individual sized flourless chocolate tortes for dessert.

"Oh, wow!" Sarah exclaimed, eyeing the spread. "This all looks so delicious." Her stomach growled in response, causing her to cringe.

Jared laughed. "I guess your belly agrees. Take a seat. And a toast first." He poured the champagne as Sarah sat cross legged facing him.

He handed her a plastic flute, saying, "Excuse the fine crystal. This packed better."

She chuckled and held the flute aloft.

He touched his glass with her and said, "To us, mi'lady. May this be the first of many dates."

Sarah smiled. "To us," she echoed.

They maintained eye contact as they took their first sip, but then got distracted by Whiskey, who had finished his dinner and was now slurping some water to wash it down. Then he circled in place twice before plopping back down into a ball and tucking his snout under his front right leg.

Jared motioned to the food and told Sarah to help herself so she mounded chicken and coleslaw on her plate. She waited for him to fill his own plate and then she thanked him for making such a feast. The first bite of chicken salad electrified her taste buds: just the right amounts of savory and sweet and crunchy. Delicious.

In between bites, they discussed what they could do to protect not only Ginger but other owners of businesses from Richard Clarkson and others like him. By the time they got to dessert, they had the start of a plan. They would have Ginger use a still from the security footage and any other photos they could find to notify the restaurant associations to which she belonged to be on the lookout for him. Jared and Sarah, along with the help of Emily and her friends, would start posting on social media and Reddit, warning others. They discussed the messaging, as they didn't want to be sued for slander or defamation, so they knew they could only stick to facts that they could back up with links.

By the end of the date, Sarah felt reassured that they could be proactive. They could strike before Dick made his next move and maybe pre-empt the attack. And then, if the police could figure out a way to charge him, maybe because of all of their actions, they could stop him for good and he'd never be able to sue someone falsely ever again.

Jared said, "And maybe, just maybe, he'll be forced to pay all of those people back."

"Maybe," Sarah said, but she didn't hold out much hope about that.

She and Jared packed up the picnic as the sun started to set. Jared pulled two flashlights out from his backpack and handed her one. Whiskey led the way back home, this time without his nose to the ground so much. Sarah and Jared were quiet as they walked, the flashlights illuminating tree roots and other things that may have caused them to trip in the dark. Halfway through the forest, Sarah reached for his hand and held it the rest of the way.

When they got to her front door, they stopped. Sarah debated asking him in. But the moment was disrupted when Whiskey scratched his paw on the door.

"He's anxious," Jared said.

"Yes," Sarah said, unlocking and opening the door so he could run in. "Raccoons and other enemies of his come out when it is dark. He prefers to have nothing to do with them."

"Makes sense. Raccoons can really damage a dog or any animal for that matter."

"Yes. He's been attacked before. Dr. Schank even diagnosed

him with raccoon-induced PTSD. We don't want to go there again."

"I understand. Well, goodnight, Sarah. I enjoyed hanging out with you tonight." Jared brought her hand to his lips.

Sarah smiled and thought, *We can do better than that.* She stood on her tiptoes and planted a soft kiss on his lips. "Thank you, Jared. And thanks for including Whiskey on our date. But you may have opened a can of worms. He may expect me to cook him gourmet meals every night after this."

Jared laughed. "It was my pleasure. Pleasant dreams." He bent and brushed her lips with his before walking toward his car.

Sarah stepped into her house, shut and locked the front door, and leaned against it. *He really is an incredible guy,* she thought.

CHAPTER EIGHT

On Sunday afternoon Ginger and Sarah sat together for an hour and hashed out all of the places and food service-related organizations Ginger needed to notify about Richard Clarkson's con. Ginger promised to provide photos to Jared and Sarah by the end of the day on Tuesday so they could start their social media warning campaign. A coordinated effort seemed the best strategy, and Sarah reached out to local lawyer Moose McCabe to review the messaging.

On Wednesday afternoon, Gladys stopped by Carter's Canine Coiffure and asked Sarah if she and Whiskey would go with her to visit Kahlo and Cassatt on Thursday after work. Sarah opened the schedule book and took a look.

"Sure," she said. "We have a light afternoon. We could leave as early as three, if that works for you." Sarah eyed Emily to see if she was listening. Emily was clipping the nails of Iggy the iguana while his human Taylor cringed with each snip.

Emily nodded her head at Sarah and mumbled, "Whatever we have, I've got it. It's why you pay me the big bucks," and then she giggled.

"Very funny," Sarah said. To Gladys, she said, "We'd love to go with you."

"Perfect. I'll be outside at three. Thank you, dears." Gladys walked out the door.

"Em, do you, um, want to get...um...some coffee after work?" Trevor asked.

Emily pushed a ringlet of her blue hair from her line of sight using the back of her hand that held the clippers as she held Iggy with her other hand. "Yes, but I only have half an hour. My mom's expecting me home for dinner."

"Cool." Taylor looked more relaxed, like he was relieved to have asked and gotten a yes.

Sarah smiled to herself as she turned her back on them. She glanced down at the schedule, only one more client to see today and they should be walking through the door at any minute.

But instead of Daphne and her French bulldog, the next person who walked through the green door of the Coiffure was Janice Jenkins. "Hello, Sarah. Whiskey. Emily," Mrs. Jenkins said. She was dressed as she often was in a pastel tweed suit and wore sensible beige half-inch block heels.

"Hi, Mrs. Jenkins," Sarah said. She never could get used to calling her Janice.

"Hi, Mrs. Jenkins," Emily said. "Nice to see you."

"And nice to see the both of you and this fine looking lizard." Mrs. Jenkins reached a sun-spotted hand toward Iggy and stroked his side.

"This is Iggy and his human Taylor," Emily said. "Taylor, meet Mrs. Jenkins."

"It's an honor, ma'am." Taylor said, putting out his hand to shake Mrs. Jenkins' hand. Taylor, as well as much of the town, had taken part in the search parties for Mrs. Jenkins a few months before.

Mrs. Jenkins shook his hand, and then she said, "Sarah, if you will," and walked toward the door.

Sarah went through the opening in the counter and followed her next door neighbor, with Whiskey close at her heels. When they stepped out onto the porch, Mrs. Jenkins said, "I've gotten a call and must leave town for a few days. Maybe a week. Will you get my mail and watch my house?"

Recently, Sarah had been given a key to Mrs. Jenkins' house as she had to travel to make some restitution for her past. "Of course," Sarah said.

"Use your key to bring the mail inside and to check on things."

"No problem."

"Thank you. I will text you when I know more about when I'll return."

"Okay. Do you need a ride to the airport?"

"No, dear. Bill has that covered." She looked at the elegant gold watch on her wrist. "We leave in twenty minutes."

"Safe travels." Sarah gave her a hug, and they parted ways. Sarah and Whiskey went back inside, but not before Whiskey took a pee break in the front yard.

On Thursday afternoon, Gladys was as punctual as Big Ben. Sarah said goodbye to Emily and thanked her for locking up before she helped Whiskey into the backseat of Gladys' Camry. It was an above average temperature so Gladys slid Whiskey's window down so he could hang his head out as they drove. He smiled his cattle dog smile at the drivers they passed, and this made Sarah and Gladys laugh. A number of the people they passed returned Whiskey's smile.

In no time at all, they had made it to the big white farmhouse. Once again they were surrounded by poodles before Gladys had shut off the engine. Whiskey jumped through the open car window and joined the pacing pack.

"Whiskey, that's not how we get out of cars," Sarah said. "Have better manners."

He shook his head, either at her or because a fly buzzed him, Sarah wasn't sure. And then he took off running with his friends. Gladys grinned, watching them go. "Such joy," she said.

Sarah wondered where Daisy and Donovan were since the last time they greeted them in the yard. "Should we knock on the screen door?" she asked.

"I guess so," Gladys said. She started up the steps and then said, "Hello, anybody here? It's Gladys and Sarah. Oh and Whiskey."

They waited on the outside of the screen door, listening. But they heard nothing.

"Maybe they are in the barn," Sarah suggested. "You wait here. I'll go look."

"I called them and told them we were coming," Gladys reiterated.

"I know you did. Maybe they can't hear us. I'll be right back." Sarah hopped off the porch and jogged around the house to the barn. The door was wide open and the light was on so Sarah went inside. In the first stall were both poodles who seemed thrilled to see her. "Hello, girls," Sarah said. "Have you seen Daisy and Donovan?"

Kahlo ran to the door and scratched at it, and her sister followed.

"I'll be with you in a minute. I have to find the humans."

Sarah did a cursory inspection of each stall and the only barn inhabitants she saw were the two poodles, though she was sure there were spiders and mice somewhere. She raced back around the house to Gladys who was still on the front porch. "Any luck?" she asked.

"No," Gladys said. "Something doesn't seem right."

Sarah pursed her lips. "Your dogs are anxious to see you, but I think we need to find Donovan and Daisy first." Sarah put her hands around her mouth to create a megaphone and yelled their names. Then she and Gladys listened.

Faintly, Sarah heard a moan from inside the house. Without waiting for an invitation, she yanked open the screen door and went in. "I'm coming," she said. She went through the living room and started down a hallway and a moan was louder. Gladys followed closely on her heels.

A bathroom on the left had a light on, an open door, and a blue-jeans clad leg visible. Sarah popped her head in and declared, "Oh no," before taking three steps into the room. Daisy was on her side. Her skin was printer paper white, her breathing sounded shallow, and she had clearly been vomiting. She moaned as Sarah bent over her. "Daisy, Daisy, what happened?"

Daisy's eyes fluttered open and then shut again. She tried to push off the floor to sit but collapsed from the effort. Her mouth formed a word, but no sound came out.

From behind Sarah, Gladys said, "I think she said Don."

Daisy moaned again.

"I'll see if he's in the house," Gladys said, leaving Sarah with Daisy.

Sarah touched Daisy's skin, which was clammy but also hot. She wondered what was wrong with her. But her thoughts were interrupted by Gladys' scream. "Sarah, come quickly."

"I'll be back in a sec," Sarah said.

Sarah ran from the room and looked in each open door from the hallway until at the very end, in the master bedroom, she found Gladys and Donovan. He was perfectly still on the bed and his coloring was gray-white. Gladys had her mobile phone to her ear.

"Is he—" Sarah started to ask.

"He's still breathing but barely." Gladys gave the address to the nine-one-one operator and told them to get here as fast as possible and that the poodles were friendly.

"You stay with him. I'm going back to Daisy," Sarah said.

She sat on the bathroom floor and held Daisy's hand and told her the paramedics were on their way. Daisy didn't respond. It was the longest ten minutes of Sarah's life waiting for emergency services to arrive, but when the Parks walked through the bathroom door followed by a menagerie of dogs, they brought with them a glimmer of hope.

After both Daisy and Donovan were loaded into the ambulance and had set off for the hospital, Gladys asked Sarah, "Now what?"

"Well, we don't know how long they will be gone, and someone has to take care of these dogs," Sarah said.

"Should we check with their neighbor? Maybe they have kids or someone that should be notified?"

"Maybe," Sarah said. "None of their neighbors are that close by as people here have acreage, but I can go see."

Gladys rubbed her hands on her arms like she was cold or had a sudden chill. "Or maybe we should just wait here for a while or call the hospital or something."

"How about if you go out to the barn and spend some time with your poodles? I'll check with the neighbors and join you once I return. Come on, I'll walk you out there. They were so excited to see me. I'm sure they will be elated to see you."

Sarah walked with Gladys through the back door of the farmhouse to the barn and Whiskey and the poodles followed them. She opened the door for Gladys and helped her slip inside the stall, keeping Whiskey and his friends out. To them, she said, "Dogs, I need to run next door. You stay here and keep watch."

All but one standard poodle and Whiskey followed her command and sat outside the stall door. Whiskey and the poodle trailed after Sarah as she jogged the long driveway and down the street to the next closest house, a ranch style on what she estimated was five acres. As they approached the white front door, a cacophony of barks erupted from within. "Pipe down!" a male voice shouted.

The door opened before Sarah had a chance to knock. The man was wiry and had salt and pepper hair weighed down to his skull by grease. He was flanked by four standard size gray poodles. "Yes?" he asked.

The poodle with Sarah gave one sharp bark to the dogs on the other side of the door. Whiskey emitted a friendly whine. "Hi. I'm Sarah Carter. I was next door at Daisy and Donovan's and they have taken ill and have gone to the hospital. My friend is getting two dogs from them and it's only our second time visiting. We wondered if you knew if they have children or anyone we need to contact."

As the man's poodles tried to push past him to get out the door, Sarah wondered why poodles were so popular on this street.

The man commanded his dogs to sit, and they responded like marines to a drill sergeant. Whiskey and his poodle friend sat, too. To Sarah, the man said, "Something happened to Daisy and Donovan? Oh no. That's terrible. I hope they get well soon. But no, they don't have kids, so I don't know what to tell you."

"Okay," Sarah said. "Do you know who takes care of their dogs when they go out of town?"

"They never go out of town," the man said.

"Oh." Sarah felt her eyes widen in surprise. "Okay then."

"Their whole lives revolve around those dogs and their land."

"Oh, okay. Thank you for your time," Sarah said. She noted that he never gave her his name and that he didn't seem particularly friendly.

He shut the door, and as Sarah and the two dogs started down the driveway, she felt like she was being watched and turned around. The curtain moved to the left of the front door.

As Sarah walked back to Daisy and Donovan's she considered what she needed to do. She couldn't abandon the dogs. Maybe she and Gladys should stay for the night. When she got back to the barn, she told Gladys what the neighbor said and ran the idea of staying there by Gladys, who admitted she had been thinking the same thing.

"I can call Bill. He has a key to my house and can get my medicine and stuff I'll need," Gladys said. "Maybe he can bring it to me. I will call him."

"While you do that, I'll feed this pack some supper."

"Okay, dear," Gladys said. "Bring some out for my girls, too."

"I will." Sarah nodded. The kitchen was as immaculate as the first time they were there. She felt a bit awkward going through the cabinets looking for kibble, but she was grateful all of the bowls were still atop the counter. Sarah wasn't sure how much food to put out or what the environment needed to be like to feed everyone without fighting and to make sure every dog got his or her fair share, but she made her best educated guesses.

She dropped off a bowl for mama dog, close to her head. Once again, her babies were feeding from her belly. She gave the standard poodles the big bowls at the far end of the kitchen and the smaller poodles little bowls closer to the fence with mama dog and her pups. Whiskey she fed by himself near her feet as she wasn't sure if the dogs would be territorial in their own house. Once they all had licked everything clean with no skirmishes, Sarah took two small bowls, one for each dog, to Kahlo and Cassatt.

"Bill said he'll bring my stuff and he's packing a bag for himself, too. He doesn't want me to stay alone, and we think you should head back to town. You've got a business to run tomorrow and who knows how long it will be before Daisy and Donovan will be discharged."

"It's no problem, Gladys. Whiskey and I can stay," Sarah insisted.

"It's unnecessary. Just help me make sure a guest room is made up." Gladys opened the stall door and shut it behind herself. "I'll be back to walk you around the yard after you eat, girls." She pointed to the leashes hanging on a hook by the door. "I just keep thinking how fortunate it is we showed up when we did. I don't know what's wrong with them. But I'm not sure Donovan would have made it."

"That crossed my mind, too. And before we check out the guest room, I want to check out that bathroom," Sarah said.

"You take care of that. I'll go to the bedroom."

"I didn't mean I have to go," Sarah chuckled. "I was thinking it might need some cleaning. Daisy was pretty sick. I want to make sure it all went into the bowl."

Gladys nodded her head. She waited in the hallway while Sarah flushed the toilet and used a paper towel and some diluted cleaner to wipe around the toilet and to wipe down the bathroom counter and sink.

They found a guest bedroom next door to that bathroom. Its queen bed wore a chintz bedspread and crisp looking sheets. "We'll stay in here," Gladys said.

Sarah smiled at the thought of Gladys and Bill cohabitating.

When Bill arrived twenty minutes later with two bags slung

over his shoulders and a paper sack of groceries, Gladys handed Sarah the keys to the Camry and told her to drive Whiskey safely home. She'd collect her car once Donovan and Daisy returned. Then she and Bill each hugged Sarah and Whiskey goodnight.

On the drive home, Sarah mused how she loved that in her town neighbors took care of each other, even if they didn't know each other very well. Emergencies really could bring out the best in people.

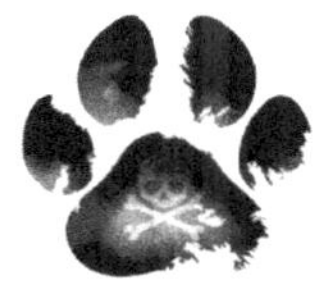

CHAPTER NINE

On Friday morning, with Whiskey riding shotgun, Sarah drove the Camry to Gladys' house and parked it in her garage using the automatic door opener clipped to the visor. Though Cottageville crime rates were low, Sarah figured the Camry was better off inside than it was sitting in front of her house. Sarah texted Gladys to let her know and received the response: "All good here. Poodles just finished breakfast. Bill is making us eggs and toast. Heard anything about D and D?"

Sarah responded that she hadn't checked in at the hospital but planned to around lunch time. "I'll let you know what I find out," she texted. She and Whiskey walked the couple of blocks from Gladys' house to Java and Juice and were surprised to see people occupying only two tables. Sarah wondered where everyone was.

Whiskey walked slowly to the counter with Sarah trailing behind. She wore a steely blue shirt with three cartoon cattle dogs on the chest. Over the dogs were the words "Red Heelers" and under the dogs were the words "Heart Stealers".

"Love the shirt," Ginger said. She was working the register today, and Jared was nowhere in sight.

Sarah wondered if he had mentioned he was traveling and she had forgotten. She didn't think so, but they had only texted a few times since their date. "Thank you," Sarah said. "Didn't you give this to me?"

"Maybe. I've bought so much dog-related apparel for you, I can't remember all of it." Ginger smiled and reached for her BFF's to-go tumbler. "Are you buying a pastry and salads or just the black coffee?"

"Do you have any of those delicious tequila and lime chicken salads today?" Sarah eyed the glass pastry case. "And two chocolate croissants, please."

"I made the salads this morning. We have those and barbeque chicken, in addition to vegetarian ones."

"I'm sticking with my original choice." Sarah grinned.

"It's a good one," Ginger said. The salad had slivers of tortilla chips, black beans, and cojita cheese.

Sarah looked around the cafe one time before leaning forward and telling Ginger what happened when she and Gladys and Whiskey went to visit the poodles.

Ginger's eyes were huge like spotlights and her face blanched. "That's awful. Are they okay? What do you think is wrong with them?"

"I don't know. His shallow breath is what throws me. I mean the flu could make you weak and vomit-y and hot and clammy at the same time. Neither of them was well enough to talk. But he was barely breathing and that doesn't scream flu to me."

"Pneumonia?" Ginger raised her eyebrows.

"Doesn't that make you wheezy or raspy because of the fluid in your lungs?"

"I think, but I'm not sure."

At that moment the door opened and the bell attached to it tinkled. Whiskey ran to meet the newcomer. Sarah turned around just as Ginger said, "Hi, Wendy."

Wendy Parks walked up to the counter with Whiskey wiggling at her heels. She greeted Ginger and Sarah before saying, "I'm so glad you and Gladys called us when you did, Sarah. You may have saved their lives."

Sarah's heart floated in hope. "Are they okay?"

"Daisy is better. They gave her something to stop the nausea and they are rehydrating her. We dropped someone else off at the hospital an hour ago so I checked on them while I was there. Looks like she'll make a full recovery."

Sarah's heart took a dive. "And Donovan?"

"Well, he's in intensive care and in a coma. His vitals are better than when we brought them in, but—" She stopped talking and grimaced.

"Do you know how they got sick or what they have?"

Wendy shook her head. "They weren't well enough to talk so we went with standard procedure: oxygen, fluids, monitor heart rate, and temperature. I'm sure the ER ran labs so they'll look for the cause of illness."

Ginger asked, "Do you mean like white blood cell count and things?"

Wendy nodded. "Yes, that and narcotics, drugs, toxins."

"Wow. I hope Donovan's going to be okay. He seemed like a nice guy. Is Daisy in a unit where she can have visitors?"

"Yes. She's in room 211."

"Thanks for letting me know. I'll go in a few hours. I gotta run right now. I'm so glad I ran into you, Wendy. Thank you for everything you do for this town."

"It's our pleasure." Wendy's smile glowed from within. She took Sarah's place at the counter and placed an order, as Sarah and Whiskey exited Java and Juice.

"I'll race you to the Coiffure, Whiskey," Sarah said, taking off with long strides, and trying not to allow the coffee to burble through the hole in the top of the tumbler.

Despite his shorter legs, Whiskey blew past her and ran down the sidewalk giving it his all. The white tip of his tail pointed like an arrow behind him. He reached the green door of the Coiffure at least thirty seconds before Sarah and turned around, sat, and waited for her.

"Well done!" She praised him, and then opened the door so he could enter. Sarah tried to catch her breath as she walked the salads and pastries to the counter. "Good morning, Em. And how are you today?"

"Just dandy. You raced your dog again. When are you going to learn that he will always win? He's the Usain Bolt of cattle dogs."

Sarah laughed. "He is. You're right. Here's a chocolate croissant and our lunch." She handed the Java and Juice bag to Emily and then Sarah walked through the opening in the counter into the back room. She covered her clothing with a dark denim apron patterned all over with two-inch gray paw prints and wrapped the ties around her waist and gathered them into a bow on her belly.

Emily put the salads in the fridge and placed the croissants on paper napkins. "They must still be warm. The chocolate is all gooey."

"Yum," Sarah said, picking up hers and taking a bite. She made a small, happy hum as she chewed the buttery pastry and rich and dark filling.

Emily threw a dried chicken treat to Whiskey, who caught it in the air and then retreated to a corner to eat. Then she inhaled her croissant like it was oxygen to her soul. "So good," she said when she finished and wiped the chocolate that had coated her lips.

Just as Emily was about to read aloud the morning schedule, the Coiffure's front door opened and in walked Officer Candace Grimes in full uniform.

"Hey, Whiskey," Candace greeted him. He met her with a wagging tail and a grin. "Sarah. Emily. Good to see you, too."

Sarah lifted the counter and walked through the opening. "What's up?" she asked. While she and Candace were friends who got together occasionally, Officer Grimes was petless and had no use of the Coiffure's offerings.

"First," she said, smiling at Sarah. "I want to know how you keep ending up in the action of weird things that go down in this town."

Emily said, "She's got you, Sarah. Maybe you're the cause, not the savior." Then Emily laughed as if that was the funniest thing she had ever heard. A beat later, Emily's brows furrowed. "Wait. What did I miss? What happened?"

Officer Grimes said, "I heard you and Gladys called nine-one-one on the poodle rescuers."

"Yes, we did. Gladys is still there, and Bill is with her. We don't know them well, but someone had to step up and care for those dogs."

"That's so kind," Grimes said. "And just another reason I love this town."

"What happened to the poodle rescuers?" Emily asked. There had been no messages on the town's social media page.

"They were sick. Very sick," Sarah said. "So, like Candace said, Gladys called emergency services, and the Parks came and took them to the hospital. I'm running over there, to the hospital, during lunch to check on them. I need you to hold down the fort here."

"No problem," Emily said. "What kind of sick were they? I mean what was wrong?"

"I don't know. Wendy said something about blood work and tox screens this morning." Sarah looked at Candace for confirmation.

"Standard blood panels when things aren't obvious."

"How long do those take?" Sarah asked.

"Normal blood work for blood cell counts and stuff is quick. Narcotics and other drugs, usually twenty-four hours. Toxins can take weeks, and often they have to know what they are looking for to be able to find it."

"Oh wow," Sarah said. "I asked Chief James to check for allergens in that orange."

"Yeah. It's gonna take a while," Candace said. "Anyway, I just wanted to stop by and razz you but also see how you're doing. You've had a crazy couple of weeks." She touched Sarah's arm.

"I'm fine. I'm concerned about Donovan being in a coma. Wendy said Daisy is doing better. Gladys said she can stay as long as she needs to. I'll let Daisy know when I see her today. At least that's one less worry for her."

"If you need anything, either of you, you know where to find me," Candace said. "Oh, and the second thing I wanted to mention is I am thinking of getting a pet. You know what my life looks like with shifts and overtime. What do you think is best for me?"

"A fish," Emily said. "Super low maintenance."

Candace chuckled. "And not very cuddly."

"True," Emily said. "Though you could get those kind that they have in Japan and Thailand and Korea that eat the dead skin from the bottom of your feet. That looks so cool. I saw a short documentary on it."

Sarah shuddered at the thought. "Are they carnivores?"

Emily's eyes rolled to the ceiling like she was trying to remember the answer. Then she grabbed her phone from her pocket and searched for the answer. "Hmm," she said. "Never mind. Turns out those *garra rufa* fish are starved so they will eat the dead skin from your feet. They are usually plant eaters. Humans are horrible. So mean and devious to other species and their own." She had tears in her eyes as she put the phone back in her apron pocket.

Sarah said, "Humans do suck sometimes. But for a pet, you could pick a rodent of any kind, a hamster, gerbil, guinea pig, rat. Any of those can be cuddled but also will survive on their own for hours. Cats will, too."

"Or an iguana or another kind of lizard," Emily said. "Or—" Her eyes lit up. "You could adopt a bunny. Pat at Cottageville Animal Rescue has some great ones. She brought a Holland lop in at the beginning of summer for a nail trim. It had the sweetest, scared face."

Candace said, "I like the idea of a rabbit. A neighbor got me one for my fifth birthday and I loved that bunny so much." She grimaced like she ate something unsavory before she said, "One day a raccoon worked its way into Peanut Butter's outdoor pen and killed it." She shivered. "I've hated raccoons ever since."

Emily said, "That's awful and totally understandable. Get a new bunny and keep it inside. You can litter train it. They are great pets."

Sarah added, "Raccoons, for all their furry cuteness, can wreak a lot of havoc. Whiskey certainly doesn't like them."

Whiskey's ears radared at the sound of his name.

"So I guess that's settled then. I'll go see Pat and rescue a rabbit. Thank you both for your feedback." Candace scratched Whiskey's ears on her way out the door.

Sprinkles the twelve-pound shih-tzu and her human, Hannah Beau, Cottageville's first female fire chief, entered just as Candace was leaving. The two women said hello while Whiskey sniffed his small black and white friend, who wiggled her butt in response.

Emily took Sprinkles from Hannah. "Oh, her ear fur has gotten long and has a little mat," she said, stroking a tiny knot of fur at the bottom of Sprinkle's right ear.

"I know. I know," Hannah said. "I got too busy and her hygiene got neglected." Hannah and her husband, Hunter Byrd, had adopted twin girls from China earlier in the summer and their lives went from a two person, one dog household to four humans and a dog overnight. Everyone was still trying to adjust, especially since the girls were five and curious and engaged and trying to understand the language and life in a household in America as opposed to an orphanage in GoaZhou.

Sarah asked, "How are things going with Bao and Ai?" Before the girls had arrived in Cottageville, much of the town threw a shower for Hannah and Hunter. Carole Binds, the town librarian, gifted them with children's books in Chinese and English. Various neighbors gave them dresses and jeans and cute tops and tights and all of the things girl children might want to wear. The martial arts studio offered three months of free lessons to the girls, the local Chinese restaurant offered free egg rolls for their first six months in Cottageville, and a number of people pitched in to get the girls white, wooden princess bunk beds with matching pink and white comforters, pillows cases printed with golden crowns, and glass slipper sheets. Hannah had cried when she saw the outpouring of love and gifts.

Her face softened, and her eyes emitted love like a torch did light. "They're fabulous. Such a blessing. Totally worth the two years we waited for them. Bao lost her first baby tooth two days ago. Now Ai can't wait until her tooth starts to wiggle and falls out."

Emily chuckled. "Did the tooth fairy do her job?"

"Absolutely. Except I had to check online what the going rate is these days."

"I'm sure it is much more than when we were five," Sarah said.

"It certainly is. She's paying five dollars per tooth now."

"Wow," Sarah said. "I had no idea. That's inflation."

"Yep. I've gotta get to the station. One of you, text me, please, when Sprinkles is ready. Thanks." With that, Hannah took off.

Emily took Sprinkles to the wash tub, while Sarah and Whiskey greeted Max the malamute. They usually only saw him once or twice a year as malamutes stayed clean and wore down their own nails. But Max's human Gregor White had texted that he needed an emergency appointment. Max had rolled in something super nasty that had embedded into his fur. Sarah could smell the gray and white dog as soon as Gregor opened the door.

"Max, what on earth did you get into? Smells like rotten eggs and old cabbage—"

"And horse dukey," Gregor interrupted. "I think he went next door and decided to coat himself in our neighbor's compost pile."

"And you didn't want to hose him off yourself?" Sarah asked, smiling, as she knew a hose alone would not clean the compost or whatever from Max's many layers of coat.

"He clearly needed professional care."

Max hung his head like he was ashamed of the odor he was emitting.

"Come on, bud, let's get you in the tub and shampooed." Sarah led the eighty-five pound dog to a walk-in tub and turned on the water. "I'll text you when he's clean again."

"Sounds good. And thank you for fitting us in," Gregor said.

Two and a half hours later, Sprinkles was done and had been picked up, and Max was playing with Whiskey while he awaited the arrival of Gregor. Emily clipped the nails of a maltese while its mom waited in the entry area of the Coiffure. If Sarah was going to head to the hospital to check on Daisy, now seemed to be the best time.

"Mind if I run out for an hour, Em?" Sarah asked.

"Go ahead. I've got things covered."

"Thanks," Sarah said. "I'm going to leave Whiskey with you."

"Yes, of course. Don't try to take him to the hospital." Emily picked up the right paw of the maltese and inspected the nails one by one before cutting any of them.

Sarah removed her apron, checked her hair in the bathroom mirror, and added a smear of lipstick before telling Whiskey, "Stay with Em. I'll be back soon." She patted his head.

The hospital was a seven-minute walk, and as Sarah approached she noted that the parking lot was only partially full and no ambulances sat in front of the ER doors. *That's a good sign,* she thought. She entered through the big glass sliding doors and said hello to Fred the security guard.

"Hi, Sarah." He tipped his hat to her. Fred had a pug that had come in a couple of times when it was having flea problems.

"How's Bug?" Sarah asked.

"The same. No, actually, he's gained two pounds that Dr. Schank wants him to lose. But you know Bug, he's not exactly keen on going for walks or other types of exercise."

Sarah smiled. "You could try cutting down on his kibble and replacing half of it with a bit of green beans and low-fat cottage cheese. That would give him fiber and be filling but would have fewer calories. Just a thought."

"That's a great idea. Thanks."

"You're welcome. Let me know if it works."

"I will. Thank you."

Sarah said goodbye and made her way to Daisy's room. She knocked twice on the wall though the door was open just so she wouldn't catch Daisy by surprise. The woman was still pale, but her coloring was better than it had been last night. As Sarah approached the bed she wished she would have brought something with her as a gift.

"Hi." Daisy smiled. "I believe you saved my life."

Sarah grasped Daisy's hand that was atop the white sheet. "I'm glad to see you are better."

"Feels like I was hit by an eighteen-wheeler. I don't know what happened but this reminds me of the one time I got food poisoning."

"I'm sure the doctors will figure it out," Sarah said, gently squeezing Daisy's hand. "I'm glad Gladys and I were able to help. And speaking of which, did you know she and a man named Bill, who lives here in town, are staying at your place and caring for the dogs?"

Daisy's eyes teared and she nodded her head. "Gladys called here a couple of hours ago to let me know. She is so sweet."

"She is. Bill is, too. He didn't want her to be alone. But don't worry about home yet. Focus on your health and regain your strength. Vomiting repeatedly zaps our energy. It's awful. I know." Sarah grimaced, remembering her own experiences.

"It really is," Daisy said. "They want to keep me until tomorrow. Just to make sure I'm okay and rehydrated." She tilted her head towards the IV bag attached by hosing to her arm. "Donovan...well, I don't think he's faring so well." A tear slid down her cheek, and she let go of Sarah's hand to wipe the tear away.

Sarah wondered if she should admit to knowing Donovan was in a coma. "Wendy said they are keeping him stable. I'm sure he'll recover. He just may need more time. He was sicker than you were."

"He was. He got sick first, and I was trying to care for him, but then it hit me, too. Such a weird flu or whatever. One minute we were fine. We fed the dogs, did some gardening, ate some lunch, and went out to repair a piece of equipment in the barn, and the next thing I knew Donovan was pale, said he might faint, but then threw up in a bush outside the barn."

Sarah's eyes grew wide. "Did he actually faint?"

"Not then, but he wasn't too steady. Every few steps he vomited as I tried to help him and hold him up from the barn to the house. Once I got him in our bed with a bucket next to him, I went outside and hosed all of the areas where he vomited. I didn't want the dogs getting into it."

"That was smart," Sarah said.

"Then I checked on him and it seemed like he fell asleep, though he was hot and sweaty. I emptied the bucket. It was bile by that time. And cleaned it out and put it back against the bed in case he needed it when he woke up. I went to the kitchen to make a cup of tea after all of that. And right after a few sips, I started to feel too hot, like I was overheating, and the room spun a little. I ran to the bathroom and made it just in time. Over and over I got sick, as you could probably tell. Since you found me. I couldn't even pick myself off the floor. I had no idea how Donovan was doing by then. I called to him as best I could. My voice wasn't loud after all of that. But he was silent."

Sarah said just above a whisper, "Yes, he wasn't breathing very well when Gladys found him. It was why she called the medics." Sarah paused and frowned. "Do you think it could have been a severe case of food poisoning from your lunch?"

"I don't see how. We had leftover chicken from dinner the night before. I cut it and made sandwiches from it on bread I made myself. And we each ate an apple. Oh and a piece of banana nut cake. It was delicious."

"Sounds like a good meal," Sarah said. "So a flu?" She didn't believe Daisy and Donovan did drugs.

"Maybe," Daisy said. "I just don't know." Her eyes welled with tears again.

Sarah patted her hand. "Do you want me to bring you a book to read? Or do you need anything?"

"Just for both of us to be well. I miss the dogs," Daisy said.

"I'm sure you do," Sarah said. "The couple of times I've been apart overnight from Whiskey since I got him almost seven years ago drove me crazy. The bed I was in seemed so empty without him next to me."

Daisy smiled. "I know just what you mean. Thank you, Sarah, for stopping by, and to you and Gladys for making sure everything is fine with our pack."

"That's what neighbors do," Sarah said. "Oh, and speaking of which, I met your next door neighbor. I went over to see if you had family who needed to be told you were here. He's..." Sarah paused searching for the right word.

"A bit gruff," Daisy supplied with a small knowing smile.

"Exactly," Sarah said.

"He's always been that way. But I think his bark is worse than his bite. He breeds poodles, did he tell you that?"

"No, he didn't. But at least four barked at me from the door."

"He's always been super crabby, but I'd like to think that anyone who works with dogs can't be all bad, right?"

"Probably not," Sarah said. "Dogs are the best judges of character. Whiskey certainly is."

"I agree. Well, thank you for coming by. It was very nice of you. And again, thank you for saving both of us from...whatever that was."

Sarah could see Daisy's eyelids droop. "Get some rest. I'm glad you'll be able to go home tomorrow. Good-bye."

Daisy's eyes were closed before Sarah left her room.

She debated asking the ICU nursing staff how Donovan was but figured since she wasn't family they would not tell her. Instead, she made her way back to the Coiffure wondering what exactly had happened to Daisy and Donovan.

CHAPTER TEN

As Sarah walked through the big glass automatic hospital lobby doors, she almost collided with Moose, who was looking down at a folder in his hand as opposed to where he was going.

"Hi, Moose," Sarah said.

He was wearing one of the six or eight suits he seemed to have on rotation. Today's jacket and pants were a medium gray with blue pinstriping, and underneath his jacket he wore a coordinating pale blue dress shirt, open at the collar. "Sarah. You were on my list of people to contact today. Look for an email from me later. I have reviewed your wording and made some suggestions as to how to avoid getting charged with libel."

"Thank you," Sarah said, glad she could move ahead with her plan to warn others about Dick.

"Has Ginger received any demands or been served with anything yet?" Moose's brown eyes looked into Sarah's. He reminded Sarah of a spider contemplating a fly that had landed in its web.

"Not that I know of. But you really think it is coming?"

"Based on everything you sent me, it seems like a sure bet."

"Even though he knows the police were on the scene?"

"He knows there was nothing he could be charged with."

"But if he files a suit or makes a false claim..." Sarah's voice trailed off.

"Then he could be a heap of trouble. But so far, it looks like everything has been to his advantage." Moose's mouth was in a grim line, but his eyes sparkled like he considered a countersuit his idea of a good time.

"True. But he's never come up against us, here in Cottageville." Sarah stood taller and put her balled fists on her hips.

Moose grinned showing his bleached, Chiclet-sized teeth. "Exactly. Good running into you. Look for the email. I've gotta go. Last will and testament needs to be signed." He took wide-legged steps towards the elevator whose doors opened just as he got to it.

When Sarah returned to the Coiffure Whiskey greeted her by throwing his front paws up against her jeans and stretching as tall as he could. She leaned over and kissed his nose. "I'm so glad you love me, boy." She scratched behind his ears.

"Learn anything?" Emily asked. A corgi named Coco Chanel was in the wash tub. Her fur was full of suds. She tilted her head, eying Sarah.

"Hello, Mademoiselle Chanel. How are you today?" Sarah asked, on her way through the hinged counter.

"She smelled of dog as opposed to No. 5," Emily joked.

"*Mon Dieu,* we can't have that." Sarah chuckled and donned her apron. "Daisy doesn't know why they got sick. It looks like she'll go home tomorrow. I ran into Moose and he said I'll receive an email later today with the wording for our campaign against Dick Clarkson."

"Oooo, that's good news. I can't wait to get started on that. Let's make him regret that he ever came to Cottageville." Emily's eyes glinted like diamonds catching the light.

"So maybe after we work a half-day tomorrow we can throw a Disable Dick party. What do you think? I can see if Jared and Ginger are available after they close at two."

"So much fun," Emily said. "But Travis asked me to go to a movie tomorrow so Sunday would be better for me. Could we do it then?"

"Absolutely. I'd never want to interfere with your love life," Sarah teased. "I could never compete with the two T's."

"Very funny. But seriously, I'm not sure if it's a date or we're hanging out as friends." Emily rinsed Coco Chanel, swishing the water through her fur, washing away all of the suds so only wet dog remained. Then she wrapped the dog in a plush tan towel that Sarah handed her.

"How did he ask?" Sarah refilled a smaller shampoo bottle with a gallon jug.

"He texted."

"Hmm. Tone can be difficult to discern from a text."

"Exactly," Emily said.

"What did it say?"

"We were texting about our favorite movies and then he texted, 'want to see a movie at the theater on Saturday late afternoon?' and I responded, 'Sounds good'."

"What are you seeing?"

"I'm not sure."

"Is there a specific movie you'd like to see?"

Emily shook her head, which did not disturb her purple spiked hair in the least. "I'm not even sure what's playing, to be honest."

"Ahh, so you're more interested in spending time with him," Sarah said.

"Can you blame me?"

"Not at all. I'm going to look at what's showing while you coif Ms. Chanel." Sarah pulled her phone from her apron pocket and browsed the cineplex that was closest—a twenty-five-minute drive to a bigger town. She read aloud through the listings and declared she wasn't familiar with any of them.

"Me neither," Emily said. "And it doesn't really matter. I'll see whatever."

Sarah laughed as she said, "It's more about the popcorn?"

"Yes, and the overpriced Junior Mints." Emily raised her voice to carry over the blow dryer. "And sitting in the dark with a guy wondering what he's thinking and if he's going to hold my hand or put an arm around me and if he's really paying attention to the movie on the big screen or paying attention to me sitting next to him."

"Wow. You captured the first movie date so vividly."

Emily shrugged. "I just voiced what we all go through."

"Yes, you did. It's been so long since I've been to a movie with anyone. Mostly I stream."

"We all do. But it's not as magical as being there...even if the place is packed."

"That's true." Sarah ate a bit of her salad since she went to the hospital instead of taking a lunch break. She only got two bites in when the Coiffure door opened, and Sascha ran in pulling Barbara Order behind her. Whiskey raced to greet his favorite German shepherd friend. They circled around twice snout to butt before breaking and slipping underneath the counter and into the back room. Sascha's leather leash trailed after her.

"That dog," Barbara exclaimed, readjusting her boobs in her fitted tank top that matched her royal purple yoga pants. "She couldn't wait to get here and pulled me so hard my girls popped out."

"At least you're married to the chief," Sarah joked. "I doubt he'd arrest you for indecent exposure."

Barbara grinned. "James is a big fan of the girls, if you know what I mean. He's a T man, not an A."

Emily's jaw dropped at Barbara's comment but she recovered quickly.

But before Emily or Sarah could respond, Barbara said, "I'm going to be late for class. Text me when she's done," and then she went through the door.

"That was more than I wanted to know," Emily said. "Now anytime I see the chief, I'm going to flash back to that moment. Gross." She wrinkled her nose.

"Definitely TMI," Sarah agreed. "Come on, Sascha, let's remove your leash and collar and get you in this tub." She opened the walk-in tub's door and waved the dog inside.

Whiskey stood on his hind legs with his front paws on top of the tub. He gave one slurp to Sascha's muzzle, as if to let her know he'd be waiting while she had her bath.

"Those two." Emily smiled. "So much love." She ran a brush through Coco Chanel's fur one last time, before tying a red satin bow on her collar, and securing it around her neck. "Now you're ready for the catwalk, Coco. Though your legs may be shorter than the other models." Emily set the corgi on the floor, where Whiskey gave her a sniff.

"You're too funny, Em," Sarah said, working her shampoo-filled fingers into the black and brown fur of the shepherd. "So what are you wearing tomorrow for your date or not-date?"

Emily shrugged. "Probably the usual. Doc Martens, jeans… why?"

"Travis is fairly fashionable."

"That is true." Emily looked at the schedule to see who they were expecting next.

"So you don't want him to be dressed nicer than you."

"Also true. Maybe I should change my hair color tonight. You know, something more glamorous, like Marilyn Monroe blonde." Emily grinned.

"That would certainly be a change." Sarah reached around to Sascha's tail, making sure she had suds the whole thing. "But it also wouldn't seem like you."

"I'm not starlet material? I don't have presidential appeal?"

Emily struck a pose like she was trying to hold her imaginary skirt from uplifting in a draft, and she jutted her bottom lip into a pout. In a breathy voice she said, "Mr. President..."

Sarah shook her head. "You crack me up. You can look and be any way you want to be. But the Em I know and love has her own unique style. Wear a dress with your combat boots or platform or wedge Vans. Dye your hair black or red or hot pink or whatever you want. Just don't conform to some external notion of sexy or attractive or whatever. Travis, and Taylor for that matter, like you for you. Because you're hilarious and a badass."

"Wow. Thanks for the pep talk, Tony Robbins. I will unleash the power within. Ha ha ha. I do think I will change my hair color tonight. It's been purple long enough, and besides I only did it for Oodle. What color are Gladys' new dogs? Never mind, I'm joking."

Sascha was rinsed so Sarah and Emily worked on toweling off her topcoat and undercoat as best they could. Then Sarah started the process of blow drying the dog while brushing out her loose fur, which clustered in light-as-air clumps that floated through the Coiffure. Whiskey tried to grab one with his mouth as it passed by his head but the blow dryer burst of hot air was faster than his snout. Chasing after it amused him for a minute until he finally caught the tuft in his powerful jaws.

"He's eaten worse," Sarah exclaimed.

"All dogs have," Emily said, as the Coiffure door opened and Coco Chanel's human Braidington Bradley popped his head into the opening. "Is my darling ready?"

Braidington's close cropped wiry black hair gleamed with pomade or hair gel. His eyes were the color of melted milk chocolate and his cheek bones jutted enough to make the sides of his face to his chin into planes. Sarah thought he was the most beautiful man she had ever seen. But she thought he was probably gay. *I mean, what straight man would name his dog Coco Chanel,* she thought.

"Braidington, Coco is clean and bowed and ready to go," Sarah said, welcoming him into her business with a smile.

"Perfect," he said, coming more fully into the room. He wore a black suit and a white button down shirt, open at the neck. Sarah was sure his clothes and shoes were worth more than her old Jeep.

Coco Chanel ran to him as fast as her little legs would permit her to go, and he bent and scooped her into his arms. "Such a beautiful girl," he said, nuzzling her clean, soft fur with his chin. With his free hand he reached into his pocket and pulled out a bill and handed it to Emily. "Thank you so much, both of you," he said to Sarah and Emily. "And you, too, Whiskey." He flashed a snow-white smile and then turned and left the Coiffure.

"Wow," Emily said after he closed the door. "Did that just happen?"

"I believe so," Sarah said.

Emily glanced down at the paper money in her hand. "He gave us a hundred, Sarah. That's a hefty tip."

"It's all yours, Em. You made the first lady of fashion look her finest."

"Gee, thanks, Sarah. I appreciate that. Now I can afford to buy Twizzlers and Raisinettes at the movies, too." Emily grinned.

Sarah finished up Sascha and then texted Barbara that her dog was ready while Emily clipped the nails of a couple of walk-ins. Sarah then texted to confirm their three appointments for tomorrow, before they called it a day.

Sarah wished Emily happy hair dying before she locked up and they parted ways. On the walk home Sarah planned her evening, including reviewing Moose's suggestions and inviting her friends to Sunday afternoon's Operation Disable Dick, which she wanted to host at her house and provide pizza, salad, and beverages for anyone who wanted to help stop that despicable man.

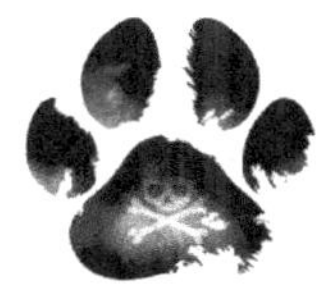

CHAPTER ELEVEN

Just as Sarah, Emily, and Whiskey were saying goodbye to their final canine client of the day, the green door of the Coiffure opened and two small poodles on skinny leather leashes entered followed by Gladys and Bill.

Gladys wore a pastel tracksuit over a floral t-shirt, and Bill wore his usual button down shirt and jeans.

"Sarah," Gladys started, "I know you are closing soon, but I wanted to ask for a favor. It's too soon after the girls' surgery to bathe them, but when Daisy was released from the hospital this morning, she told me to take them home with me. And I would but they smell like barn."

Sarah smiled. "I have just the thing." She opened the counter and motioned for Gladys and Bill to bring the dogs through.

Emily finished the transaction with Merlin the maltese and his human dad, while Sarah picked up Kahlo and Cassatt one by one and set them on the counter. She removed a packet of dog grooming wipes from a drawer and handed Bill and Gladys one wipe each. Sarah showed them how to start at a poodle foot and work their way up one leg and then another. When their wipes were gray from dirt and grime, Sarah gave them clean ones. Steadily, Gladys worked on the front of Kahlo while Bill cleaned the front of Cassatt. Sarah alternated between dogs and took care of their back ends, careful not to touch their bellies or undersides.

"This should at least take most of the barn smell from them. But make an appointment for them in ten or twelve days and we'll trim their nails and give them proper baths," Sarah said. "How did Daisy look? And any change with Donovan?"

Gladys ran a wipe around Kahlo's neck and said, "Daisy's coloring is back. Her cheeks had some color. She's still a bit weak, which is why I agreed to take the dogs now. She'll have her hands full with the others. Donovan is out of the coma. She said she got to see him before she was discharged. He's not well. But he is breathing on his own and awake."

"That's at least good," Sarah said. "Is he still in the ICU?"

"He is. But they said if he could handle some liquids and a soft diet today, they may move him to a regular room tomorrow. Daisy is hopeful about that."

"That's good news. If you think Daisy needs any help this afternoon or evening, Whiskey and I could drive out there."

"That's sweet of you, Sarah, but she said her best friend had agreed to come stay with her until Donovan gets home. That's who drove her home from the hospital. A lovely woman named Cherie who lives in Cedar Rapids." Gladys finished cleaning Kahlo and asked Sarah to set her down on the ground.

Bill had one more ear to wipe on Cassatt. "They still don't know what made them sick." He shook his head like he couldn't believe it.

Emily shoved her apron into the washing machine before popping into the bathroom to change clothes and to add a slash of plum stain to her lips. When she emerged in an all black babydoll style dress that coordinated perfectly with her now-raven hair and her combat boots, Bill eyed her from head to toe and raised one eyebrow.

"Yes, I have a date." Emily grinned at him.

"Good for you, honey," Bill said. "You look nice."

"Thank you. Gotta run or I'm gonna be late. I'll see you tomorrow, Sarah. Goodbye, Gladys. Good to see you, Bill." Emily rubbed behind Whiskey's ears and he smiled at her. Then she exited the Coiffure.

Gladys and her new housemates, Bill, Sarah, and Whiskey soon followed. Bill drove Gladys and her poodles the few blocks to Gladys' house while Sarah and Whiskey cut through the park on their way home. After they passed the playground that vibrated with the sounds of children laughing, climbing up jungle gyms, and swinging as high as they could on swings, cheered on by parents and caregivers, Sarah and Whiskey spied Coco Chanel running as fast as her little legs could carry her after a ball. Sarah looked up to see Braidington holding the blue plastic handle of a Chuckit! She was surprised to see him in shorts and a t-shirt, standing in the grass in his bare feet. And she was even more surprised to see John Beams standing next to him, similarly attired. Sarah had rarely seen John in anything but his uniform, and she didn't know he and Braidington were friends.

Whiskey trotted across the expanse of grass to greet them, and Sarah had no choice but to follow. Braidington threw the ball hard and it flew through the air more than a dozen yards. Whiskey picked up speed and caught it in his mouth before Coco Chanel could run the distance. He pivoted and ran the ball back to his friend and dropped it at her feet.

"Whiskey, nice catch!" John praised him. He approached Whiskey and scratched behind his ears.

Whiskey smiled up at John.

"That was one graceful capture," Braidington said."Give me five."

Whiskey raised his right paw and hit Braidington's outstretched cafe au lait colored hand.

"Sorry about that," Sarah said, catching up to them.

"Nothing to be sorry about," Braidington said. Coco flattened herself in the grass at Braidington's bare feet, as if she had had enough ball chasing for one afternoon. Whiskey licked her ear but he remained standing and at attention, like he hoped to chase the Chuckit! ball again.

"Are you on your walk home?" John asked Sarah.

"Yes. Moose gave us the language to use to notify the restaurant associations and to start a social media campaign warning people about Richard Clarkson and his lawsuits, so Ginger and Jared and Emily and I are meeting tomorrow afternoon to start the letter writing and posting. I figured you and Chief James should know...just in case there's any backlash."

"Good to know. Thanks. Oh the lab said they'll have the results of testing the orange next week."

"Oh nice. Maybe we should have started a pool, a friendly wager," Sarah suggested.

John laughed. "We already did at the station. Five dollar buy-in."

"Hey, is it too late to get in on that?" Sarah reached into her pocket and pulled out a five.

"Grimes started it and is the bank. Ask her. I'd let you in, if it was me." John smiled at her.

Braidington said, "Five bucks. That's chump change. A c-note would have made it more interesting."

"Of course it would. But we're on cop salaries, not your fancy money manager one." John touched Braidington's forearm in a way that Sarah read as affectionate.

Sarah looked from John to Braidington and back to John again. *Wait*, she thought. *Are they on a date?* Just past where the three of them were standing was a plaid blanket topped by two pairs of male sandals, a picnic cooler with bottles of beer emerging from its zippered top, and an unopened bag of barbeque chips.

"Come on, Whiskey, we should head home. We have stuff to do. So nice running into both of you. And you, too, Coco Chanel." Sarah crouched to pet Ms. Chanel.

"Good to see you, too, Sarah," John said. "And seriously, see if Grimes will take your money." He grinned at her.

"I will. Thanks. My guess is peanut allergy," Sarah said.

"I think the chief took that one, too," John said.

Braidington said, "Too easy. Could not even be a food allergy. My money would be on cat. Way more rare and unexpected."

Sarah's eyes widened. "That can be as dangerous as peanut allergy. John, are they testing all allergens or just foods?"

"I would think all, but I should probably confirm that." John pulled out his phone, maneuvered his index fingers around the keyboard, and shot off a text.

"Anyway, good day to you both." Sarah motioned for Whiskey to come with her, and they crossed the rest of the grass to the other side of the park. Whiskey ran at the geese on the bank of the pond and scattered them amid squawks and wing flapping waddles. And then he circled back to Sarah's side, which is where he stayed the rest of the walk home.

On their street, Sarah and Whiskey stopped at Mrs. Jenkins' house for her mail, since she was still away. Sarah placed the mail inside a paper bag that rested by a coat rack in the entryway of her own craftsman bungalow since she didn't have Mrs. Jenkins' key on her. Whiskey ran ahead of her and into the kitchen where she heard his metal tags clanking against his water bowl. Sarah poured herself a glass of water and removed a bag of organic greens, a carrot, a bell pepper, some turkey pepperoni, and crumbled feta from the fridge. She chopped the veggies and threw together a salad with olive oil and balsamic for lunch.

As she ate, she searched on her computer for more information about Richard Clarkson, including his previous known addresses again and his phone number, just in case they needed those things. Sarah took notes on the legal pad next to her laptop. When she discovered his LinkedIn profile, she felt like a slot player whose machine was chiming and lighting up and clanging with a jackpot. Richard Clarkson had a degree in chemistry and spent more than two decades as a researcher for the big pharma company. When she looked up the company, she learned that they made the allergens for scratch tests. "Holy cow!" Sarah said aloud.

Whiskey picked his head up off the floor where he was resting and gave Sarah an inquisitive head tilt, ears angled forward, eyes that pierced her heart.

"Better than a clue in a mystery novel," Sarah declared to Whiskey. "I mean seriously. Real life is so much weirder than fiction." Sarah copied the link to Clarkson's profile and dropped it into a message for Chief James with the heading, "Look who knows all about allergens…because it is most likely his job!"

Then she copied the same link and message and sent it to Emily, Jared, and Ginger. And just in case Ginger was handed a lawsuit, Sarah sent the same message and link to Moose in case he needed to prepare a response or defense on Java and Juice's behalf.

Sarah stood up and stretched, and then took her salad bowl into the kitchen to rinse it and put it in the dishwasher. She added water to the kettle on her stove and got down from the cupboard her favorite cattle dog mug, one Whiskey had allegedly asked her parents to buy for her from him last Christmas. It had his photo and the words "Roses are red. Violets are blue. Thanks for the belly rubs and for picking up my poo. Love, Whiskey" on a white background. She smiled every time she saw it. To the mug, she added an Earl Grey teabag and waited for the water to come to a boil.

Once the tea was made, Sarah returned to her laptop and notepad.

She decided to make a spreadsheet of all of the places Dick had sued, along with the owners' names, addresses, and phone numbers, and any other pertinent information. She got the spreadsheet set up, just as her phone rang.

"Good afternoon, my lord," Sarah answered.

"Mi'lady. I received your text. And that intrigued me to do some snooping of my own."

"Most excellent," Sarah said. "Did you find anything? Would you like to snoop from here? I created a spreadsheet but have yet to populate it. This is how I'm choosing to spend my Saturday afternoon into evening."

"Then we have similar ideas," Jared admitted. "And yes, I would enjoy volleying ideas with you, if you and Whiskey can stand my company two days in a row." Playfulness and hope oozed through Jared's voice.

"You're our favorite tall comic book creator, barista, and picnic partner. We love your company." As soon as the words flew from Sarah's mouth she questioned her use of the word love. *Was it too much, too soon? At least she didn't say she loved him.*

Jared's chuckle relaxed Sarah's nerves. "Then I'll be by soon. Prepare to share your wi-fi password and that spreadsheet."

"Will do." Sarah disconnected and sat staring into space for a beat. Then it hit her that Jared was on his way and that she smelled like she had worked with wet dogs for part of the day, because, well, she had. She raced into her bedroom, while stripping off her jeans and t-shirt and underthings, and stepped into the shower. A quick scrub, shampoo, and shave later, she moisturized and dried off and then donned white jeans and a "Life is Better With Dogs" emerald green t-shirt. After all, she had never met a day that wasn't improved upon by wearing fun, dog-related apparel. Just as she buttoned the jeans, the doorbell rang and Whiskey ran, barked, and slid across the hardwood floors into the front door. Sarah was surprised to see Jared, too, looked freshly showered, with his hair still wet and the smell of Irish Spring surrounding him. He grinned upon seeing her and gave her a hug. And Sarah felt her heart hammer at quad espresso speed.

CHAPTER TWELVE

Three hours later, Sarah and Jared called it quits on the spreadsheet. They had nineteen lawsuits listed. They weren't sure they had found them all, but they were tired of looking as it was as tedious as trying to find a flea on a black Lab and they hated the thought of spending any more time on The Dick, as they both now called him. "I can't believe one person has done that much damage in so many places," Sarah said, closing her laptop as if she was trying to contain the destruction to people's livelihoods.

"I wonder how he chooses the towns and the cafes or restaurants."

"Maybe we should plot the places on a map," Sarah suggested. "Just not right now."

"That's a good idea, but yes, let's do that tomorrow. I'm as exhausted as a rabbit chased by a greyhound." Jared stood to stretch his legs. He moved his arms in big circles from his shoulders.

"You okay?" Sarah asked, standing, too.

"Too much time today hunched in front of the computer. It's not very ergonomic."

"Definitely not," Sarah agreed. "I think we should DoorDash some Chinese food. Unless you want to go out somewhere."

"What? And leave Whiskey? I think not, mi'lady."

Whiskey perked up at his name and thumped his tail twice on the floor.

"I'm sure he'd love some dinner. In fact, why don't I do that and here—" Sarah thrusted her phone with the app open into Jared's hand. "Order us some egg rolls and kung pao chicken, moo shu pork, and whatever else you think we should eat. Oh and a six-pack of Tsingtao, if you're up for it. My card is already saved in my profile. It's my treat."

"I'll be sure to tip well," Jared joked.

"I always do," Sarah said from the kitchen while opening a container of Whiskey's raw, human-grade dog food.

"I know you do, Sarah." Jared came into the kitchen, carrying the water glass he'd been using. "All ordered. They said thirty minutes. And you're right, beer sounds great." He looked down at Whiskey who was inhaling his food. "Yo, Whiskey my man, you might want to savor that food on the way down so you don't have to taste it on a rebound."

Sarah chuckled. "He's always been an eager eater. Even as a young pup."

Whiskey licked his bowl clean as Sarah said that.

Jared helped himself to more water from the tap in Sarah's kitchen. As he passed her, he brushed against her shoulder, and Sarah once again caught a whiff of Irish Spring soap. She wanted to hug him and breathe in the soap and Jared's natural scent. Being near him felt grounding the same way walking in the woods did or being embraced by her favorite blanket or sweater. Sarah wondered if he felt it too.

"Want to watch a movie or something?" Sarah asked, leading the way out of the kitchen and into the living room.

Sarah sat one-third of the way from the left arm of her sofa, with her feet propped on her coffee table, in front of the television, hoping and trying to encourage Jared to sit right next to her.

He did.

"Can I put my feet up, too?" he asked. Gray Bombas socks covered his feet and lower legs.

"Of course," Sarah said. "Make yourself comfortable."

She turned on the television and said, "Prime, Netflix, or Max. Those are the choices unless you want to stream from the net. Want to watch anything in particular?"

"Have you watched *Magic for Humans?*"

"Nope. Have you?"

"Only an episode or two. It's really good, and I'd love to talk about it. I can't figure out how Justin Willman does half the stuff he does. Do you mind if we watch it?"

"Not at all. What channel?"

"Netflix."

Sarah pushed that button on her remote and waited for the app to load. Whiskey jumped onto the sofa next to Jared. He circled once, putting his butt against Jared's thigh and his head on the arm of the sofa. "If he's in your way, tell him to get down," Sarah said, shaking her head at her intrusive dog.

"He's fine," Jared said. He ran his hand over Whiskey's rump, ruffling his fur. "Aren't you, boy? You just wanted a better view of the magic."

The show started and Sarah said, "Oh wow," and "How does he do that?" a number of times during the twenty-four minute episode.

"No idea. But I want to know. We need to figure it out," Jared said. "It's like another mystery we could solve."

The doorbell rang and Whiskey flew off the couch barely missing the coffee table as he darted, barking, to the door.

"I'll get it," Jared said, his long legs taking him halfway to the door before Sarah had the chance to stand and move. She shrugged and wandered into the kitchen to get a bottle opener and her collection of painted wood chopsticks, a couple of plates, and a fork, as she didn't know if Jared used chopsticks or not. This was their first foray into Chinese food together.

They ate in the living room, with Whiskey curled against Jared, as they binged a couple of more episodes of *Magic for Humans* before Sarah let the television enact its screen saver.

After her final bite of kung pao chicken, Sarah set her plate on the coffee table and said, "I love how every episode has a theme. That seems like a great way to organize the show."

"It is. But how in the hell does he put someone's wedding ring or phone or other personal item inside a glass jar? That's way different than a sleight of hand card trick."

"Maybe..." Sarah's voice trailed off as she wrinkled her face and pursed her lips in thought. "But isn't it all sleight of hand though. Isn't that what magic is? It's tricks and distraction and illusion. Not unlike what Dick tried to pull at Java and Juice. He probably never considered we'd connect the dots to the orange and that Whiskey would find it in the restroom."

"Or that we'd know he injected something into it and himself. Because we are almost certain that was the case."

"Exactly. He figured the cafe was busy. You and Ginger were distracted and all of the other patrons were, too. No one would notice the trick he was about to pull until he was ready for an audience to witness his feat." Sarah's eyes widened and she shook her head. "Black magic, for sure."

"But we stopped him, Sarah, and soon we will know what he took to create the reaction. I do find it strange that someone would play Russian roulette like that though." Jared put his own plate and chopsticks on the table and turned slightly so he was facing Sarah with his back to Whiskey. "Thanks for the Chinese food. It was really good."

Sarah crossed her right foot atop her left knee so she could sit facing Jared. "Maybe he doesn't look at it that way. I mean, he's a scientist, right? Maybe he figures he's calculated everything down to... well, a science...so he sees little risk."

"Maybe. He's had at least nineteen lawsuits where he hasn't died. But constant allergen exposure might make allergies worse. Or does it make them less severe? I just remembered that when you go for allergy shots it's diluted regular exposure."

"I don't know if it makes them worse or better, the frequent or semi-frequent exposure. We could Google that or ask a doctor."

"It probably doesn't matter. What matters to us is stopping him from suing Ginger and Java and Juice and stopping him from doing this to others."

"I agree," Sarah said, finishing the last of the beer in her bottle.

"Besides my computer, what can I bring tomorrow?" Jared asked.

"Nothing. I'll throw together a salad and order pizzas. I have flavored sparkling water and wine and tea and coffee. I think we're good."

"What about dessert?"

Sarah shrugged. "I've got some fruit."

Jared chuckled. "I'll bring something chocolate or something leftover from Java and Juice tomorrow."

"Sounds good. Thank you," Sarah said.

Jared stood and grabbed his empty bottles and some of the cartons of leftovers and took them into the kitchen. Sarah followed him with the plates, chopsticks, and serving utensils. Whiskey remained curled on the couch with one eye open watching them.

"Thank you for inviting me to work with you and dine with you, mi'lady," Jared said, as he gathered his computer, notebook, and pens, and put everything into his backpack.

Sarah held out an imaginary skirt and curtsied. "Twas my pleasure, my lord."

Jared slipped a strap of his backpack over one shoulder and grinned at her. Sarah saw a certain sparkle in his eye as if she amused him. And she wasn't sure if it was the bit of beer in her system or the way he made her feel like a puppy that wanted to play and play and play, but she stood on her tiptoes, tilted her head, and gently pressed her lips against his smile. Jared's smile faded as his lips puckered against hers as his arms encircled her, bringing her closer to him.

Sarah closed her eyes and leaned further into the kiss. She opened her mouth slightly and enjoyed the touch of their tongues.

But Sarah suddenly jolted. She felt off balance—and not because of the kiss—and pulled back.

Whiskey had refused to be excluded from the affection so he had inserted himself between Jared and Sarah, bumping into their legs and ultimately parking himself on their feet. When they looked down at him, they found him grinning up at them, flashing his black gums and small teeth.

"Do I need to ask for your permission, boy?" Jared joked. "I believe it was she who initiated the kiss with me."

"Most definitely," Sarah said. "And we don't need his permission. Though it does seem we have his approval."

Jared's chuckle resonated from deep in his chest. He bent and scratched the fur around Whiskey's ears. "You're the best dog in Cottageville. Yes, you are. You know that, right?"

Whiskey gave one staccato "woof" of yes.

Sarah shook her head, bouncing her ponytail. "Did you drive here or walk?"

"Walked."

"Oh." Sarah had thought she could leave Whiskey in the house, walk Jared to his car, and kiss him again without an interruption.

Instead, Jared said, "Well, I should be going. I look forward to seeing you tomorrow, Sarah. Whiskey, I need my feet back so please move."

As Whiskey walked toward the living room, Jared leaned down and kissed Sarah for a split second. Then he turned and walked out the front door.

Sarah turned the deadbolt and headed into the living room to have a chat with Whiskey, who was lounging on a sofa with his eyes closed. She sat next to him and stroked his thick dark ginger fur. "I like him, Whiskey. I know you do, too. And I know it's been just you and me for a long time and that I haven't dated much since we moved here. But sometimes I will need some human time, without your supervision. You understand, don't you?"

He opened one eye and stared at her. And then his mouth pulled back slightly into a smile before he licked her forearm.

"Thank you, love. Thank you for understanding."

Whiskey pawed Sarah's thigh twice like he was assuring her it was okay.

She hugged his neck and then asked, "Do you need to go out before we get ready for bed?"

In response he went airborne off the sofa before running to the back door. Sarah jogged after him and opened the door.

Whiskey patrolled the fence perimeter with his nose to the ground before doing his business and re-entering the house and heading straight into the bedroom. He circled the duvet into a nest atop the bed, curled himself into a comma, and closed his eyes.

"At some point, we may need to rethink these sleeping arrangements," Sarah murmured, pulling an extra blanket out of the cedar chest since Whiskey had commandeered the duvet.

He snored in response.

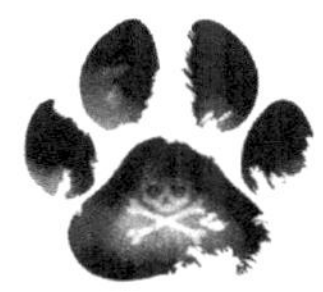

CHAPTER THIRTEEN

With her hair in a ponytail and wearing an old University of Washington t-shirt and gym shorts, Sarah spent some of Sunday morning catching up on housework after an early morning walk. She cleaned both bathrooms, vacuumed the whole house, and dusted the living room. Then she scrubbed down the kitchen before putting together a big salad of leafy greens, walnuts, slices of strawberries, and feta.

At noon, a knock on the front door sent Whiskey running and barking in reply. Sarah popped the salad into the fridge and dried her hands on a dish towel before following her dog. Janice Jenkins stood on Sarah's porch. She wore jeans—which Sarah didn't even know she owned—Reebok sneakers, and a pastel blue sweater.

Whiskey wagged his tail and sat for a scratch of his ears, which Janice provided with a "Good boy."

"When did you get back?" Sarah asked. "Would you like to come in?"

"An hour ago, and no, I just stopped by to tell you I have returned from Spain."

"I hope your trip went well. Everything was fine at your house. Let me grab your mail." Sarah left the door open and walked two feet to the table to the right of the entryway. On it was a paper bag of Janice's newspapers, small packages, and correspondence. "Here you go." Sarah passed the bag to Mrs. Jenkins.

"Thank you. And yes, the time went better than expected. I was able to pinpoint and help them correct some flaws in their security." Janice nodded her head. "They have a few more tasks for me to do, but won't be ready until the fall, so I'll go back then."

"That sounds exciting." Sarah's mind raced in a Grand Prix of questions, but she knew the work her octogenarian neighbor was doing was top secret so no answers could or would be provided.

"It is and I'm grateful to have all of the secrets behind me and to be able to use my 'little grey cells' as Hercule Poirot referred to them. It helps keep me sharp." Mrs. Jenkins' smile lit up her slightly wrinkled face.

"We should all use our little grey cells as often as possible," Sarah said. "Speaking of that..." Sarah segued into what she had learned about Richard Clarkson and his repetitive ruses and their plan. Then she asked Mrs. Jenkins if she had any professional opinions—since she had spent her career working for the alphabet agencies of the United States government—on how to handle him.

"I think going to the associations and getting word out is a great start," Janice said. "I would think Chief James could contact the local police where Clarkson lives to let them know about the scams. I wonder how tightly controlled the inventory is at his company and if anyone has noticed some is missing. Of course we are assuming he took some from work as opposed to manufacturing his allergens in a home lab."

Sarah's eyes narrowed and her brows furrowed. "Could he do that?"

"Sure, why not? People build bombs, cook meth from cold meds and cleaning products, and do all kinds of things. If he's a skilled chemist, he could probably pull that off."

"I never even considered that."

"But you are right in the fact that he has easy on-the-job access. He may even falsify the manufacturing or inventory records if he helps himself. I'm sure it wouldn't be the first time that's happened to big pharma."

"Are you sure you wouldn't like to come in and have a cup of tea?" Sarah asked.

"No, dear. I must run. Gladys texted me a photo of her new girls so I'm going to meet them and have some lunch with her. Thank you for getting my mail and keeping an eye on the house. I appreciate it. And let me know if you run into any further problems with Mr. Clarkson. Some people in my network may find his scheme very interesting indeed."

"I will. Tell Gladys I said hello. Have a great afternoon." Sarah called Whiskey back inside and then she shut and locked the door. Sarah could smell the Windex and Pledge on her skin and she couldn't take the scent much longer. She stripped out of her cleaning clothes and stepped into her very clean shower.

Thirty minutes later, her hair had been blown dry, mascara coated her lashes and a pink gloss coated her lips, and she was attired in cuffed jean shorts and a black t-shirt emblazoned with a white outlined drawing of cattle dog wearing sunglasses and the words "official dog of the coolest people on the planet" underneath the dog. Sarah decided that it was best to do Whiskey's afternoon walk now as she didn't think they'd get the day's second walk in later. Whiskey kept his nose to the ground sniffing as they walked up their street and when they turned left and headed toward the park, he picked up his pace until he ran, barking at a crow, whose caw of disdain and flight into a nearby oak tree caused him to stand on his hind legs and jump at the base of the trunk.

"Silly dog," Sarah said. "They will never let you catch them."

Whiskey glanced at Sarah and then back up into the tree. He gave one sharp bark, then put his front feet on the ground, and trotted along his way through the green grass of Cottageville's downtown park. The playground and its jungle gym were teeming toddlers and preschoolers, running, laughing, falling, screaming, and being placated by their parents and older siblings.

Sarah smiled to herself, grateful she was childless except for Whiskey, who in human years, was older than she was. Sure, she figured someday she might want a baby...once she found a human partner...but for now, she certainly loved her life and her freedom and the peace and quiet in her house that she was sure a needy infant would destroy. She looked away from the playground to the ball fields.

Chief James flicked a Frisbee, sending it sailing through the air and Sascha sped toward the disc, jumping, and catching it in her mouth. Whiskey raced toward his friends, so Sarah jogged after him.

"Afternoon, Chief," Sarah said, huffing a bit from the exertion.

"Sarah. Whiskey. Fetch." The chief threw the Frisbee again and both dogs barrelled after it. Sascha caught it mid-air again, and Whiskey ran alongside her, his tongue hanging from his mouth, happy to tag along.

The chief threw the disc again and the dogs took off. Sarah relayed the idea Janice Jenkins had regarding someone from Cottageville PD contacting the law enforcement in Richard Clarkson's jurisdiction.

Chief James pursed his lips and narrowed his eyes before saying, "That's not a bad idea. I mean Ginger hasn't received notice of a lawsuit, but we can certainly report what happened and what was found in our... well, your...investigation." He bobbed his head twice.

"Isn't there a national database?" Sarah smiled at Whiskey, who had a ball in his mouth from somewhere and kept pace with Sascha who was returning with the Frisbee.

"Of crimes, yes. He's not been charged with one. Not here or anywhere."

"Well that sucks," Sarah said.

"Indeed. But we aren't sure he's broken a law." Chief James whizzed the disc another time and both dogs sprinted.

When they returned with the disc, Sarah noticed Whiskey was still carrying an old tennis ball with most of the fuzz worn off in his mouth. "Come on, Sascha, we gotta go. Playtime is over." To Sarah the chief said, "Barbara wants a date night so I have to go get ready. Nice running into you."

"You, too, Chief. Give Barbara my regards."

"Will do." Chief James followed his German shepherd through the park and down the path that exited on the far end.

"Have you run enough?" Sarah asked Whiskey who was now lying in the grass and working his jaw on the ball.

He considered her with his head tilted and then stood, spit out the ball, and walked back the way they had come with Sarah trailing after him. Every twenty or thirty feet, he'd lift his leg on a bush, a tree, or some grass after he sniffed it, leaving pee mail or a response for the rest of Cottageville's canines.

When they returned home, Sarah opened her laptop to the local pizzeria's website and ordered five pies. She wasn't certain exactly who was coming to her house besides Jared, Ginger, and Emily, but she wanted to make sure she had something for each person. She ordered one vegetarian pizza, one with extra pepperoni and cheese, one with mushrooms and olives, one with barbeque chicken and purple onions, and one marguerite. The website said the pizzas would arrive in thirty to forty minutes, which was approximately the scheduled time of her guests.

Sarah opened a bottle of chianti so it could breathe a little, and she pulled a stack of plates down from the cupboard, before carrying those, some paper towels, silverware, and glassware, as well as a pitcher of water awash with mint leaves into the dining room during a number of trips. Whiskey sat on the sofa and supervised her movements back and forth between the rooms.

"Some help you are," Sarah mumbled.

Whiskey cocked his head to the side, as if he was considering her statement.

After Sarah had the dining room set up for food and for working, she decided to print five copies of the emails from Moose so that each person could have a template to work from. She also printed the spreadsheets she and Jared had made so that she could assign the tasks in an organized manner. She figured if they divided the work equally, they could conquer the list with just this one get together. She was collating the stacks of papers when the front door rattled. Once again Whiskey ran to get it, though he had no opposable thumbs to turn the knob.

And he had to jump out of the way to avoid being hit by the opening door. Ginger had used her key to let herself in. Her hair was in two braids, and she wore a white t-shirt under cropped overalls and Birkenstocks. Her skin emitted the scent of sugar and cinnamon as she embraced Sarah.

"Yum. You smell good," Sarah said. "Like baked babka."

"Cinnamon rolls, actually. But close," Ginger teased. "I made ten dozen early this morning for a function at the Episcopal church, some coffee meet and greet."

"That is how you spend your day off?"

Ginger shrugged. "What can I say? They paid cash and tipped well."

Sarah grinned. "The joys of owning a local business. What can I get you to drink?"

"Anything wet with alcohol."

"Wine or beer?" Sarah asked, walking toward the kitchen. Ginger followed her as if Sarah were the Pied Piper of Adult Beverages.

"Wine, please." Ginger inspected the bottle of chianti before Sarah poured the nectar of the Italian gods into two glasses. "Random fact," Ginger said. "Did you know chianti appears in historical documents and manuscripts—the handwritten kind—from way back in 1200? I learned that in that Culinary Institute of America wine course I took."

"Those are some pretty old grapes." Sarah held her glass up toward Ginger. "To our friendship and to kicking Dick's ass."

"I'll drink to both of those," Ginger said, clinking her glass against Sarah's.

The doorbell rang and Whiskey ran so fast he slid on the hardwoods into the door with a thud.

Sarah set down her wine and raced to him. "Oh, boy, that must have hurt? Are you okay?" She checked him over before opening the door.

As soon as Whiskey spied Jared and Emily, now with the ends of her hair dyed Cookie Monster blue, he shimmied between two of his favorite people and let loose two sharp barks with his snout pointed in the air looking from one to the other. They bent at the same time to pet him, conked heads, and simultaneously said, "Ouch."

"Come on in," Sarah said. "We have wine, beer, tea, pain killers, and ice packs. What would you like? Are your heads okay?"

"I've sustained worse injuries, mi'lady, to both my head and my heart," Jared joked. He wore a black Iron Man t-shirt with faded from blue to almost white jeans.

"I'll be fine once I get some Whiskey love," Emily said, dropping her black yoga pants covered butt to the floor and throwing her arms around the cattle dog's neck. He slurped his tongue up her left cheek. "Ahh, just what the doctor ordered. I'll be good as new with one more kiss."

Sarah, Ginger, and Jared laughed. Jared eyed Ginger's glass and said, "I'll have whatever G is having. That translucent red hue is inviting."

"You really are an artist," Sarah said, "choosing a wine based on its color."

Jared grinned at her. "You know it's my secret identity cloaked under my barista apron."

Ginger said, "Dude, I love working with you. But I'm all for you hitting it big time on a movie or publishing deal."

"Me, too." Jared pulled Ginger in for a side hug. "That's why you're the best boss ever. You want what's best for me...even if it could leave you in a lurch."

"True. And don't you forget it," Ginger teased. "Especially since my birthday is next month."

"How should we celebrate?" Sarah asked, carrying the bottle of wine into the dining room. She poured a glass for Jared, before offering iced tea, flavored seltzer water, or coffee to underage Emily, who had moved into the dining room with Whiskey as her shadow.

"I may have plans," Ginger said. "I'm still figuring that out." She caught Sarah's eye and smiled.

CHAPTER FOURTEEN

A knock on the front door interrupted Sarah's snarky, "Along with a hardware store owner?" comment.

Whiskey raced to be the first to greet the newcomer, who turned out to be none other than the man in question. Daniel Snyder said, "I heard there's a take-down in progress and I didn't want to miss it." He was attired in a Buck and Son logoed button down shirt, faded black jeans, and work boots, and he carried an iPad in one of his hands.

"I welcome your testosterone in this hen house." Jared shook Daniel's hand and before stepping aside to let him enter the living room.

"I thought Whiskey had all of the testosterone Sarah needed," Ginger said, right before standing on her tiptoes and kissing Daniel's lips. "I am glad you could make it."

"Pizza, beer, and you. I wouldn't miss this for the world." Daniel hugged her before letting her go and walking into the dining room.

"I heard you say beer," Sarah said. "Is that your beverage of choice?"

Daniel eyed the wine glasses of purplish liquid as well as the bottle of chianti. "Do you have any stout?"

"Guinness, in cans."

"Perfect."

Emily addressed Daniel and Ginger, "So you guys are a thing?"

Ginger grinned. "Yes, but we've been keeping it on the DL."

Her hair stayed perfectly still as Emily nodded her head once. "Small town. Big, opinionated mouths. I get it."

"Plus we wanted to figure things out for ourselves before any outside pressure one way or another." Daniel took a pull from the can in his right hand.

"Smart," Sarah said.

As soon as they had gathered around the table, the doorbell rang. Whiskey barked as Sarah said, "Must be the pizzas."

Jared said, "I'll get it" and used his long legs to reach the door before anyone else had left the dining room. He greeted the delivery guy by name, thanked him for the pizzas, and said he'd see him tomorrow night.

As he walked into the dining room, Sarah asked, "What's tomorrow night?"

"Game night. Most Mondays for the last three or four years, a group of us, mostly guys, have gotten together to play board and card games."

"Huh," Sarah said. "I had no idea." She handed out plates to her friends and bowls for the salad, which she grabbed from the fridge, and told everyone to dig in.

"*Buon appetito!*" Emily said, raising her glass of seltzer water.

"*Buon appetito!*" The four others responded, raising their glasses and cans.

"Yeah, well, it isn't like we advertise it," Jared said, referring to game night.

"Don't want to come across as too dweeby to the ladies?" Emily joked before enthusing, "Sarah, this salad is soooo good."

"Thank you, Em. So," Sarah said between bites, "here's the plan. Ginger and Daniel will write to the professional organizations using Moose's letter suggestions to warn their members to be on the lookout. Jared will email the cafes and restaurants Dick has already sued, alerting them to everything we've learned and suggesting they contact their lawyers in case they want to counter-sue. I will work with Emily on the social media angle. Here's a copy of Moose's suggestions for each of you, along with the spreadsheets of the organizations and the restaurants and cafes. Jared and I put all of that together yesterday so we could just take action today. Let me know if you have any questions or if you have any ideas we haven't considered. And mostly, let's figure out a way to stop him from being a dick to...well...anyone."

"Cheers to that," Jared said. "And may the force of good be with us."

"Here, here," Daniel said. "But I've been wondering, why do

you think no one has pieced together before us that he's done all of these lawsuits?"

Sarah's eyes widened. It was something she hadn't considered.

But Ginger answered quickly. "They were in crisis mode, D. I know I was when he needed an ambulance while eating at Java and Juice. I'm sure the other owners and staff were, too. Plus when it is clear someone is reacting from something you served them, you feel guilty. Even if it isn't your fault. Then, when you get the lawsuit, that guilt intensifies as does the worry that word will get out and destroy everything you worked so far to build."

Daniel frowned. "Okay. I get that. But like me, you have liability insurance to cover these kinds of things."

"True," Ginger said. "We have it and hope we never have to use it. I'm sure they turned over the suit to their insurance and their lawyer and they worked together to settle it as quickly as they could for as cheaply as they could. But the owners would be all stressed out. I don't think it would occur to them to do any research about the guy. I know I wouldn't...if it wasn't for Sarah."

Sarah patted Ginger's hand with hers, but said nothing.

"I guess that makes sense," Daniel said.

No one else said anything as they turned their focus on their food and screens.

For the next two hours, in between bites of pizza and forkfuls of salad, their nails clicked over the computer keyboards in front of them. Sarah arose from the table to get everyone another round of drinks and to give Whiskey his supper and then to let him out.

At one point, Jared exclaimed, "Wow. Two of the restaurant

owners responded to my email already. They sound pissed and itching for a fight with Richard Clarkson. But, who could blame them? A guy named Sal, who owns one of the diners, sounds like a man who is gonna go see a guy, if you know what I mean. His email expressed rage as well as creative uses of some four-letter words."

"Wouldn't want to be on his bad side, especially if he's like Sal from *The Sopranos*." Sarah shivered as she remembered scenes from the show she had watched in reruns.

Emily got up and headed to the bathroom as Sarah's phone, which was sitting on the table, blared the "I fought the law" ringtone.

"What the heck—" Jared said.

"Hello, Chief James," Sarah answered.

Ginger, Daniel, and Jared quieted, stopped what they were doing, and watched her.

"Really?" Sarah exclaimed. "That's crazy."

She was quiet for a moment and then said, "Yes, thank you for calling. I'll tell the others and maybe we can provide that information in an update to what we sent out to the organizations and restaurants. Jared's started to get responses already."

Ginger waved her hand, so Sarah added, "And I think Ginger now has a response, too. Thanks so much. Enjoy the rest of your evening."

When she disconnected, she met all of their eyes. "I'll wait until Emily returns so I only have to say it once."

"Way to keep us in suspense," Ginger said, pouring herself more wine. "Anybody else want any?" She held up the bottle.

Jared accepted a splash more, as did Sarah.

When Emily walked into the room, all eyes were on her. "What? What did I miss?" Then she turned like a dog chasing its tail. "I'm not wearing TP, am I?"

"Not that we can see," Sarah said.

"You're holding up the story," Jared said.

"What'd the chief want?" Emily asked, sitting at the table, and reaching for her glass of water.

"That's the story," Jared grumbled.

"Oh." Emily shot a sheepish grin at Jared.

Sarah cleared her throat. "The lab figured out the allergen. Shellfish. Dick is allergic to shellfish. That's what he injected into the orange so he didn't get too much to kill him."

"Son of a—" Daniel started. "That's a gutsy thing to do."

"He must think he's invincible," Jared said.

"More like insane," Emily added.

Ginger pursed her lips, like she was either holding back or thinking. She scratched her head where one of her braids started. "I'm still trying to wrap my head around the fact that someone puts his life in danger to get a few bucks. It doesn't seem like he's that hard up. I mean he is a scientist with a good job. Why would he do this?"

"Adrenaline rush," Jared said. "It's like a game, like Russian roulette, or the biggest gamble. It's the rush he thrives on and the idea that he's smarter than everyone else. Think about it. Ginger is right; I doubt he needs the money. I mean look at how much he's gotten in the suits. Fifty k here, seventy-five k, there. There's not been super punitive damages against any of the places as they haven't been proven to be at fault. It's like Ginger said, the insurance companies and lawyers threw some money at it to make it go away.”

“I agree with Jared. I think this is Dick’s version of an extreme sport. He gets off on it, at least mentally and emotionally,” Daniel said. “And he’s found it benefits his bank account, so it’s a win-win-win.”

“Until he takes too much or his system overloads or the medics don’t arrive in time,” Sarah said.

“Apparently that’s a chance he’s willing to take.” Daniel took a swig from a newly opened can of beer.

“So is the chief okay if we send this information to the people we’ve emailed?” Ginger asked.

“Yes,” Sarah said. “But we can’t post it on social media. Chief James said only the associations and restaurants could know, so that if he stars in his one-man show anywhere else, they and their authorities will know what to look for.”

“Sounds good,” Ginger said, returning her focus to her laptop and the spreadsheet next to her computer.

“Hey, guys, since Sarah and I are done with social and I still have homework for my summer class to do, I’m gonna head out. Thanks for the salad and pizza, Sarah. It’s been great working with all of you.” Emily stood and put her MacBook Air in her backpack.

Whiskey stood too, waiting for her to walk toward the door. She bent and massaged her fingers around his head. “You’re a good boy. Such a good boy,” she oozed.

Whiskey smiled at her showing a hint of his teeth.

“You’ll see her again in the morning, Whisk.” Sarah stood and walked with Emily out the front door and to her black Honda CRV, which was parked in Sarah’s driveway. Whiskey tagged after them. “I appreciate you giving up your Sunday evening to help," Sarah said.

"Of course," Emily said. "Someone tries to mess with one of us, they mess with all of us. We'll take him down, Sarah. I know we will."

"It will be interesting to see how effective this campaign will be."

"I'll keep an eye on our analytics," Emily said. Then she opened the driver's side door and got into her ride. "See you *mañana*." She shut the door and started the engine.

Sarah looked up at the sky and marveled at how starry and warm the night was before she and Whiskey re-entered the house.

"Hey, Sarah," Jared said, "Sal wants the phone number for the chief to give to his lawyer. Do you think that's okay?"

"I would guess. But give the number for his office, not his cell."

"I don't have either in my phone. Can you give me the numbers?"

"Of course." Sarah sat next to Jared, pulled up Chief James' contact, and slid her phone toward him.

"Can you text me the contact, so then it's in my phone, too?"

"Absolutely." Sarah picked up her phone from the table and did as he asked. She mentally noted that Ginger and Daniel's chairs were much closer together now, and with the way she was sitting so close to Jared, it almost seemed like they were on a double date. *Hmm*, Sarah wondered, *would I want to do that? Or more importantly, if I did date Jared, would he really want to double date with his boss?* Sarah smiled to herself.

"What's that smile for?" Jared asked.

Oops, busted, Sarah thought. "Nothing," she said aloud.

"Didn't look that way." He grinned at her and jostled her with his elbow.

She figured it was best to change the subject. "What games are you playing tomorrow night?"

"Probably Risk. It's one of the guy's—who shall remain nameless and who isn't me—favorites. I think he has delusional visions of controlling the world some day." Jared chuckled.

"That could be scary. We need no more dictators."

"Agreed. I'll help you clean up," Jared offered, eying Ginger and Daniel who seemed lost in whatever they were doing on Ginger's computer together.

He picked up the plates around the table while Sarah gathered up the leftover pizza into one box. They carried the plates and silverware, empty salad bowl, boxes, and two empty wine bottles into the kitchen. Once the dishwasher was loaded and the trash thrown away, Sarah turned to Jared. "So I have read that someone at the university is giving a lecture on the works of John Byrne in a few weeks. Would you be interested in going with me?"

"Are you serious?" Jared asked. "How did I not know about this?"

Sarah shrugged.

"And how did you know about this?"

"Like I said, I read it somewhere. John Byrne won't be there. As you probably know, he doesn't travel or go to the cons much, not since 2018."

"Someone's done their homework," Jared said.

Sarah blushed. "Maybe a little. And you never answered. Do you want to go?"

"Of course I do." He picked her up in a hug and twirled her around. "Mi'lady, you surprise me—almost every time."

"Well, I figured if I was going to ask you on a date, it needed to be something spectacular."

"Color me impressed." Jared leaned down and kissed her softly on the lips. When they parted he said, "Yes, yes, yes. I will absolutely go with you. Just say when."

"When," Sarah said, grinning.

"Ha." The staccato of the syllable hung in the kitchen.

Whiskey meandered into the room to see what he missed. Jared addressed him. "Did you hear it, Whiskey? We're going to a lecture on John Byrne."

"We as in you and me," Sarah said. "He has to sit this one out."

"His loss." Jared knelt on the floor and stroked Whiskey's ears. "I'm going to hear all about how *X-Men* was created, boy. I am a lucky man."

Whiskey put his paw on Jared's knee, as if to let him know he agreed.

"It's on a Saturday in two weeks," Sarah said. "I'll send you a calendar invite if you give me your email address."

Jared whipped out his phone from his back pocket. He one-finger typed. "Done."

Sarah heard her text notification ding. "Thank you so much for all of your help yesterday and today. I appreciate it."

"Any time," Jared said. He gave her another hug. "I should be going now. Early day tomorrow."

"I'm sure," Sarah said. "Java and Juice is one of the most popular morning spots in town."

"Yes, we can't keep the wanting-to-be-caffeinated masses waiting. Otherwise, it would be a zombie apocalypse." Jared chuckled at his own joke.

"That would be a tragedy," Sarah agreed. She and Whiskey walked Jared to the door, after he poked his head into the dining room and said goodbye to Ginger and Daniel, who were now holding hands and facing each other.

Sarah brushed her lips against the scruff on his cheek when they reached her front porch. "I'll see you tomorrow, Jared."

"Until then," he said, kissing the top of her hand, and then turning and walking down her sidewalk and up the street.

Sarah and Whiskey watched him go.

When they could no longer see him, they went back inside, where Ginger and Daniel bid them a quick goodnight and saw themselves out.

Sarah set the dishwasher to run, let Whiskey out for a potty last call of the night, and then she and her dog crawled into bed with a cozy mystery story.

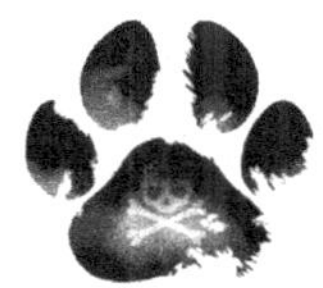

CHAPTER FIFTEEN

The next afternoon at two-thirty, Sarah's phone rang. She was mid blow-out, with the dryer in one hand and a brush in the other, of an American akita named Annabella, who stood regally with her head in the leather loop, like she innately understood she was a beautiful beast—because she was.

With the brush hand, Sarah pulled her phone from the denim and dog print apron pocket. *Ginger* was on the screen.

"Hold on a minute, *Bella*," Sarah said, turning off the dryer. She placed the phone against her ear. "Hey, beautiful human. To what do I owe the honor of your call?"

"He did it. He actually did it. And he really is a dick." Ginger's anger seethed through the phone like venom from a rattlesnake.

"Oooohhhh, you got a letter?"

"Lawsuit. Called Moose first, then Chief James, and now you."

"What'd they say?" Sarah absently brushed Annabelle.

Emily, who had finished a handoff of a yorkie to her human, motioned for Sarah to step aside. She picked up the hair dryer and took the brush from Sarah's hand. "Finish the call in the other room, and then come back and tell me all of the deets," she said.

Sarah nodded, and instead, she and Whiskey stepped outside the Coiffure. Whiskey promptly peed on the nearest azalea while Sarah stood next to her shop, listening to Ginger, who explained that Moose told her to bring the letter by, to provide the name of her insurance company, and to give them a heads up, and that he and the Chief would work to file a countersuit. But Chief James said they could now file criminal charges against him for fraud and intent to cause harm. He said they could get him for perjury too since he signed a legal document whose merit Dick knows is based on a lie. Chief James, too, wants the documents I received."

"Wow," Sarah picked at a loose thread at the bottom of her apron. "So you could counter sue for duress and libel and damages on your emotions, your business, or whatever?"

"Yes, and I'm angry enough to do so. He screwed with the wrong business owner and the wrong town."

"I know. I can feel your anger from here. And I'll match your anger and raise you some. No one messes with us and those we love." Sarah eyed a butterfly flitting toward the azalea and wished she felt as weightless. Fighting the battle against Richard Clarkson instilled a heaviness in her heart. Whiskey sat against her leg like he could feel it, too.

Ginger continued, "So he included the bill from the hospital and from the ambulance ride, bills from his therapist to deal with his trauma, and damages for not being able to work for a few weeks, mental and emotional anguish, and a bunch of other b.s. He's asking for $50,000."

"He's nuts. And you're not paying him a dime."

"Nope. Can a class action lawsuit be filed against a person?"

"Umm, not a lawyer but I don't think so."

"I was thinking after a warrant is issued for his arrest, the other cafe and restaurant owners that we emailed yesterday and I should ban together and sue him jointly."

"I like the safety in numbers thing, but don't you think it would be more exciting...and vengeful and suspenseful...for you all to sue him individually? That way he never knows when someone else is going to sue him to recoup the money they've already paid him and damages."

"Oooo, that's rich. I like the way you think," Ginger said, then she added a goodbye to someone and Sarah heard Jared's voice in the background, before Ginger added, "We have finished cleaning up for today and prepping for tomorrow. I'm going to call the insurance company, and then I'm headed to Moose's and after that to the police department."

"Are you going to call a shrink so you can start your own therapy bills to claim this lawsuit stressed you out and made you ill?"

"Ha ha. You're not far off the mark, though therapy for anger management against him would be more likely."

"That's for sure. What can I do to help and support you?" Sarah waved at Daphne who was walking Pierre across the street from the Coiffure. She wore a chambray sundress and a wide-brimmed straw hat with a white grosgrain ribbon. Daphne waved back and said, "*Bonjour, Sarah. Bonjour,* Whiskey."

"*Bonjour,*" Sarah called.

Through the phone Sarah heard Ginger say, "Hi, Daphne," and then she giggled.

"Anyway," Sarah said again, "what can I do? How can I help? Want to come for dinner tonight? Whiskey and I have no plans."

"Thank you for the offer, but I have book club at six-thirty and I'm hosting this one."

"Sounds like a fun night."

"It will be. You know we mostly drink wine and talk, right? I don't know why you won't join us."

"Eh," Sarah said. "I like to read what I like without the pressure. Plus I see Carole and Pat and the others regularly anyway."

"True. Well, I need to get going. Thank you for listening. See you in the morning. Love you. Bye."

"Love you, too," Sarah said before she disconnected. "Come on, Whiskey, let's go gossip to Emily and bring her up to speed." They opened the Coiffure door where Annabella met them, looking super fluffy and radiant. A red silky bow had been tied to her collar.

Whiskey sniffed her and nipped her lightly in the heel, which was his signal to chase him. He romped under the counter and into the back room and out again with Annabella jogging beside him, curled tail swishing proudly in the air. Happiness beamed from both dogs like a beacon from a lighthouse.

Fifteen minutes later, Annabelle's human, Drake Farmer, walked through the Coiffure's green door and both dogs raced to greet him. "My beautiful girl," Drake said, bending to hug his sable-coated akita.

"Wow, even freshly groomed she got hair all over your dress pants." Sarah handed him a lint roller. His black pants had transfer fur where Annabelle's chest made contact with his knees as he bent. He waved off the lint roller.

"The more hair on me the more love she gives me," Drake said, flashing a smile of very white teeth that contrasted with his mocha skin.

"I love your attitude. It's beautiful," Sarah said.

"For reals," Emily added.

Drake grinned. "You ladies are great and Annabella loves coming here. How much do I owe you for making her shine?"

Emily took care of the transaction as Sarah greeted Gladys who had opened the door, but did not enter when she saw the akita who outweighed her poodles by at least sixty-five pounds. "They are almost done," Sarah said, stepping outside to pet Kahlo and Cassatt, who had moved half a block up the sidewalk to wait for Drake and Annabella to leave. "How's life with the girls?"

"Eventful," Gladys said. "They are so sweet. No accidents after the first night and really, I think that was just marking the territory as theirs since they probably smelled Oodle. Just a bit of piddle on the living room rug."

"That makes sense." Sarah realized that Gladys seemed more nervous about the dog in her shop than her dogs did as Drake and

Annabella exited the Coiffure, said goodbye to Sarah, and hopped into a black five series BMW sedan. Kahlo and Cassatt ignored the big dog in favor of sniffing every blade of grass next to the sidewalk.

Emily stuck her head out the door. "Mrs. Rossmiller, did your dogs need anything? I don't see them on today's schedule."

"No, dear. They are fine. You did such a good job with them last week. I just stopped by to give Sarah the update that when I called to check on Daisy earlier today she said they moved Donovan from the ICU to a regular room. They said if he continues to show improvements, they could let him go home as early as tomorrow afternoon or Wednesday morning."

"Wow. That's amazing news. Thank you for coming by to share that with me. I could use some good news right now."

Gladys' eyes behind her glasses narrowed. "Oh, did something bad happen?"

Sarah audibly exhaled. "I guess you'll learn soon enough as I'm sure it will be all over town. That guy who had an allergic reaction in Java and Juice a few weeks ago filed a lawsuit against Ginger and her business. She found out this afternoon."

"Oh, dear. That is bad news. How is Ginger handling that?"

"Well, the police have enough to charge him with fraud as they figured out the way he caused the allergic reaction."

"Was it real?" Gladys asked, "or did he fake it?" Kahlo coughed up some of the grass she had just eaten.

Sarah bent and scooped up both dogs and cuddled their small, warm bodies to her chest so they could no longer eat the grass. "The reaction was real but self-induced." She explained all of the online research she and her friends had done and what they had pieced together and what the police and the lab had discovered about the orange.

"My, my, what a chance to take with one's own life and what an elaborate scheme. Someone with those smarts could use them to benefit society instead of running scams like a crook." She shook her head, clearly dismayed. "Sometimes I don't understand why people behave so poorly." She transferred one of the dog's leashes to the other hand and stretched out her arthritic fingers while Sarah still held the dogs.

"Greed, mostly. Though we also think he loves the adrenaline rush of it all."

"Such a shame. Well, sounds like this may be his last hurrah. I'm sure Chief James will try to lock him up and throw away the key."

"If he can. For sure, Ginger will countersue. It's just a shame that his evil intentions are costing her money."

Pat from Cottageville Animal Rescue pulled up in front of the Coiffure as Gladys and Sarah were talking. She picked up a steel cage from her passenger seat and exited her car.

Both Sarah and Gladys' eyes dilated when they spied what was shimmying in the cage. A small black wiggly nose caught their scent and the poodles in Sarah's arms yelped. A fluffy and gorgeous black and white striped skunk peered through the bars. She had a baby's clip style yellow flower barrette on her head.

"Descented," Pat said, "and her name is Petunia. Her owner died of a heart attack and animal rescue brought her to me. It's my first skunk, and I had no idea they were so sweet."

"She's adorable," Sarah said. "But the bow is a bit much."

"Makes her look like a diva," Gladys said. "She'd be a fun one to paint." To Sarah, she asked, "Can you take a picture of her when you get her inside? I'd love to try to capture her on a canvas, though I haven't held a brush much with these crooked fingers."

"Absolutely, I'll take some." Sarah bent and put the poodles back on the ground. "I'll text them to you later. Pat, do you need us to wash Petunia?"

"Oh, no, Sarah. We took care of that as soon as we got her. She actually swam in the tub. It was so cute."

"So it was you who put that barrette on her?"

Pat frowned. "Yes, but only because she came in with it on and seemed to want it back on when we finished cleaning her. She kept going over to it and sniffing it and looking at us like, 'hey, where's my flower'?"

Sarah laughed. "I've seen dogs behave that way and not want to be without their bandanas or collars."

"Yes, exactly like that. Anyway, we bathed her, but we didn't trim her nails. I wanted you to show me how much to take off before I try it myself."

"I can't stand to cut nails myself," Gladys said. "Too afraid to hit the quick when I was young and now my hands can't work the clippers." She held up her hands to show Pat what she meant.

"Those look painful," Pat said.

"Not too much, but I have some meds if it gets too bad."

"That's good, Gladys. I'd hate to think of you in pain," Pat said.

"Me too." Gladys grinned. "We'll be on our way now. Sarah, thank you in advance for texting me photos of Petunia."

"You're welcome, Gladys. Thank you for stopping by." Sarah held the door open for Pat to carry the cage inside the Coiffure.

Whiskey raced toward Pat, but he skidded to a stop when he recognized the black and white animal held inside the steel bars. A low growl voicing his unhappiness rumbled from his chest, before he took off for the back room.

"Oh cool. A skunk," Emily said, before going after Whiskey to soothe him.

CHAPTER SIXTEEN

At seven o'clock the next morning as Sarah and Whiskey took their morning stroll through the middle of town, Bill called to them from his front porch. "Sarah, could you come up here, please?"

"Sure, Bill." Whiskey beat her up the stairs though she wasn't trying to race him. He sat next to Bill and reached out his paw, like he wanted Bill to shake it.

Bill laughed and held Whiskey's paw in his hand, pumping it up and down a few times. "What a good boy you are, Whiskey," Bill said, patting him on the head and handing him a dog biscuit from the big jar that had permanent residence on his porch.

"Would you like some coffee?" Bill offered Sarah.

"I already had some. Thank you."

"Have you talked to Gladys recently?"

"Yes, she stopped by with the girls to tell me that Donovan may be coming home."

"Yes, that's true," Bill said. "But Daisy called last night after supper. Seems her friend Cherie, who was staying with her, got sick. She was so sick that Daisy had to call nine-one-one."

"Oh my. What kind of sick?" Sarah's eyes hooded with worry.

"Very similar to the way Daisy was. Daisy followed after the ambulance and asked if we would be on standby again to stay with the dogs." Bill's eyes sparkled.

Sarah wondered if it was because he felt needed...and maybe because he liked spending the night with Gladys. But she kept those thoughts to herself.

"Did you need to go?"

"Not yet. She called Gladys around eleven and said she was coming home for the night and would go back to the hospital in the morning. Her friend was stable and being rehydrated."

"Do they know why she got sick? And why Daisy and Donovan got sick, too? Could it be something in their house?" Sarah's mind flipped through scenarios: toxic mold, food poisoning, asbestos, some kind of flu, contaminated well water. Were they even on a well?

"I don't know. Daisy said they had eaten supper and twenty minutes later Cherie ran to the bathroom and started vomiting and then grew weak and couldn't leave the bathroom."

Sarah's lips grew taut. "Hmm, that sounds way too familiar."

"I agree."

"But Daisy stayed well?"

"Yes, I believe so. Gladys hasn't heard from her this morning, at least I don't think. She texted me good morning and that she'd be over later. But she didn't mention Daisy yet."

"It seems so suspicious," Sarah said.

"It does," Bill said, taking a sip of his coffee. "And since I know you like to solve puzzles and you were the one who found Daisy on the bathroom floor, I thought you might want to know about this."

"I'm glad you told me, Bill. Thank you. And please, can you or Gladys let me know if you find out anything else?"

"Will do, Sarah."

"Thank you. We must be on our way if we're going to make it to work on time."

"I understand. Have a good day." Bill reached down and handed Whiskey another biscuit for his walk home. As they cut back through the park, Sarah pondered the fact that three people in the same household had exhibited the same symptoms...but not all at the same time. What did that mean? Daisy and Donovan became ill together the first time. Cherie got sick, but Daisy did not. Sarah felt for sure that it wasn't because Daisy's immune system was super strong. *She just finished being very ill. It couldn't be,* Sarah thought. *So why else would she stay well when her friend didn't? Clearly Cherie must have done something Daisy didn't. What could it have been?*

Sarah kicked a small pebble with her foot when they hit pavement again. She watched it stay low to the ground before taking flight. That made Sarah think about flying birds and from there her mind jumped to chicken and eggs. Did Daisy and Donovan have egg laying chickens? Did they wash the eggs well before they used them?

Ginger had told Sarah a story about being on a trip in Costa Rica and getting some food poisoning from some unwashed eggs. But surely, if Donovan and Daisy had chickens they knew how to properly and safely use the eggs that they laid.

Sarah and Whiskey turned onto their street, and Whiskey stopped at every fourth bush to mark his territory. Sarah lagged behind, lost in her thoughts. When Whiskey reached their front door before her, he barked once while looking her way, telling her to hurry up.

"I'm coming," she mumbled. "Whiskey, something doesn't make sense, and this thing with Daisy and Donovan and Cherie bothers me. What if the hospital releases Donovan from the hospital today or tomorrow and he goes through the same thing again? I'm not sure he'd make it a second time. We've got to figure this out."

Whiskey cocked his head at an angle and looked at her like he was considering the possibilities.

Sarah hurried inside to put her now dry hair into a braid and to swipe some mascara on her lashes. She returned a message her mom had left her last night, confirming that yes, they could come visit her in two weeks, and yes, they could stay as long as they wanted. They were always welcome.

For the last month, her parents had been traveling around Europe and had visited Sarah's brother in Scotland, where he was a veterinary medical student at the University of Edinburgh. Sarah was thrilled her father's tech job allowed him to work from anywhere and that her mother had taken early retirement from teaching so they could explore all of the places they had talked about visiting and they could escape during all of the months Seattle was covered in gray skies and drizzle—which was three-quarters of most years.

Sarah grabbed her faithful, empty to-go tumbler and her phone, keys, and the dog leash Whiskey was rarely attached to, and called to him, "Time to go to work."

He raced from the bedroom and out the front door as Sarah opened it, and he ran until Mrs. Jenkins opened her front door to grab her newspaper. Whiskey stopped to say hello to her. "Hi, Mrs. Jenkins," Sarah said.

"Good morning to you, Sarah. And thanks again for keeping an eye on my place. I appreciate you."

Sarah smiled. "You're welcome. Enjoy the paper. We have to get to work."

"Have a good day, dear."

"Thank you. You, too." Sarah picked up her pace to keep up with Whiskey who had darted up the sidewalk and was almost to the top of their street. He didn't sniff or mark as much on their second walk of the day. He cut through the park only stopping to greet one black mixed breed dog he knew. And he waited for Sarah to catch up next to Java and Juice's red door, despite various members of their community going in and out of the establishment.

Some people greeted him by name or with a pat to the head, and then they looked around for Sarah and waved or said, "Hello."

When Sarah caught up, she said, "Thank you for waiting, but why the rush today?"

Whiskey smiled in response and waited for her to open the door for him. As soon as she did, he beelined to the counter and sat next to the person who Sarah didn't recognize who was ordering.

"Whiskey, get back here," Sarah said, pointing to the spot of floor right next to her leg.

He hung his head and crept back to her at the end of the line.

Jared's face broke into a grin as he watched them. He wore a Java and Juice logoed apron over a black t-shirt and sand colored jeans.

Sarah thought he looked great, especially when he smiled directly at her. She returned his grin.

Four more customers to go before it was their turn.

Five minutes later, Whiskey had given Jared five by tapping his paw to Jared's outstretched hand and received a homemade chicken biscuit as a reward, and Sarah's to-go tumbler had been filled with black coffee. Jared put two cilantro and lime salmon salads into a bag for Sarah and Emily's lunch, as well as two chocolate and raspberry filled croissants for them to eat for breakfast. Sarah told him she had a mystery to discuss with him, and he told her he'd be available this evening.

"I'll call you then," Sarah said.

"Or, I could bring you dinner? You get off at five?" Jared asked.

"That sounds even better. Thank you."

Jared winked at her and she grinned like a girl with her first crush. "Come on, Whiskey, I'm sure Emily is waiting." They turned and walked out of the cafe though Sarah felt more like she wanted to skip with glee…though she refrained so as not to shock her neighbors or cause them to think she had lost her mind.

When they opened the door on the Coiffure, Daphne was in the front room, handing Pierre over the counter to Em, who sported black kohl around her eyes like Cleopatra.

Whiskey trotted to greet Daphne. "*Bonjour,* Whiskey. *Ça va?*"

"*Ça va bien, merci. Et tu?*" Sarah was thrilled some of her high school French came back automatically.

"*Comme-ci, comme-ça,*" Daphne responded. "Dr. Schank had to remove a foxtail between Pierre's toes over the weekend so *nous avons été très triste.*"

"That's horrible," Emily said, "Which toes?" She inspected his right front foot until Daphne pointed to two end toes on Pierre's left front paw. A small red mark of irritation stood out against his buff colored fur. "We'll be extra careful when we bathe him and cut his nails."

"*Merci beaucoup,*" Daphne said. She adjusted the navy floral silk scarf that accessoried her plain white linen sundress. "*Á bientôt.*"

"See you in a few hours," Emily agreed as Daphne departed through the front door. Emily carried Pierre to a wash tub, and Whiskey followed at her heels.

"They had chocolate and raspberry croissants this

morning." Sarah set the bag on the back table.

"Yum. Thank you."

"You assume I brought you one?" Sarah joked. "I could just eat both of them."

"You wouldn't dare," Emily challenged, pointing the sprayer at Sarah and threatening to push the button to release the water.

At that moment Officer Candace Grimes opened the front door of the Coiffure. She wore a green tank top that showed off her muscular arms and faded blue jeans. But what grabbed Sarah and Whiskey's attention was the small, big-eyed bunny in the palms of Candace's hands. It wiggled its nose inhaling all of the scents in its surroundings, and its oversized ears drooped like a caramel colored scarf over its shoulders.

"So freaking adorable," Emily yelled above the wash water.

Sarah went through the opening in the counter and asked, "Did you get that rabbit from Pat?"

"I did," Candace said. "I followed your advice and fell in love. Who wouldn't. Look how cute he is." She held the rabbit up a bit higher so Sarah could get a better look and to make the rabbit feel safer from Whiskey. She stroked his back with her thumbs, letting him know he was safe.

"What'd you name him?"

"Maple. Pat named him and I thought that was a fine name, though not very boyish."

"Maple is a good name. But I agree with you, mostly because it sounds too close to Mabel I think. Maybe you could call him Maple Syrup or MapSyr or something to make it sound gender neutral at least.”

“Or I could have changed his name.” Candace grinned. “Unlike Whiskey here, I don’t think the mini lop knows his name.”

“Where did Pat get him?” Sarah reached out her hands asking for permission to hold him.

“She said she saw him eating some tall grass on the side of some back road. She knew he must have been a pet that was dumped or had gotten away. But no one claimed him. I first saw him the day after I was here and I fell in love. But she wanted to wait to give time for someone to say he was theirs, before she adopted him out. I picked him up last night when my shift ended. Thank you so much for the recommendation.”

Sarah ran her right hand from the bunny’s flattened forehead over its skull and down its back, and it shimmied slightly from the petting and settled deeper onto her left arm. “He’s so sweet.”

Whiskey sat in front of Sarah on his haunches, straining his head up toward the rabbit.

“Whisk, I know you think it’s a new friend, but he thinks you are big and could be a predator. Let’s give him time to settle in and feel safe with Candace before you two officially meet,” Sarah said.

“Sounds like a plan,” Candace said. “In a few weeks, I’ll invite you over and they can get acquainted. Well, I just wanted you and Emily to meet Maple. Thank you for your recommendation. I couldn’t be happier with a furry friend.”

“I’m glad you stopped by.” Sarah handed Maple back to

Candace, when a thought struck her. "Hey, did you hear that the dog rescue people where Gladys got the poodles were very ill? He's still in the hospital, but she got released. Last night, her friend Cherie, who came to stay with the woman, Daisy, ended up going to the ER with the same symptoms."

"Yes, I heard the nine-one-one call go out, plus we were notified by the hospital."

Sarah's eyes widened. "Why?"

"Because when the tox screen came back, it showed cyanide in their systems."

Sarah's head jerked back on her neck like she had been struck, and Emily's stopped mid-scrub and said, "WHAT?!?"

"Yeah. Totally suspicious circumstances…and I'm saying that as your friend and not as a cop. But yes, it piqued our law enforcement interest as well."

"Do you know where they got cyanide poisoning from?" Sarah asked. "That's what it was, right?"

"Well, we don't know about the woman yesterday, but that was definitely what showed up in Donovan and Daisy, in varying amounts, so I'm sure they put a rush on last night's blood work and tox screening."

"You'd hope," Sarah said. "But no idea where it came from?"

"We're investigating," Candace said. "But let's keep that relatively quiet for now. I do really need to be on my way. Thank you again for recommending I get a rabbit. Let's get together socially soon."

"Okay, sounds good," Sarah said.

"Bye," Emily yelled, while rinsing the suds from Pierre's short, silky fur. "Did you hear that, Sarah? Sounds like another mystery."

"Indeed it is."

CHAPTER SEVENTEEN

At six o'clock sharp, Whiskey barked from behind a fence in the side yard of Sarah's yellow craftsman bungalow as Jared walked up the sidewalk. "Hey, boy. Ready for supper?" Jared lifted a cooler higher to show Whiskey he had food.

Whiskey barked two yeses before racing as fast as his short legs would carry him around the back of the house, through the open back door, and to the front door, which he hit twice with a paw to let Jared know he was there. "You're hilarious, dog," Sarah said. "You'd think no one ever feeds you or gives you treats all day."

Whiskey cocked his head at her like, "Are you giving me grief, woman?"

Sarah opened the door and smiled at Jared. "Thank you for bringing us food."

Jared's hair was wet like he had recently showered and he smelled of piney soap and something citrusy. Sarah breathed in deeply as she loved the scent and wished she could capture it in a candle so she could smell it any time.

"Come in." She stepped back and commanded Whiskey to do the same. Jared headed straight to Sarah's kitchen and set the cooler on the counter. Then he turned to her and gave her a hug, before saying, "So, a mystery…"

"A pressing one. And I've learned more since I talked with you this morning, but I waited for you to get here before doing any research or brainstorming on my own."

"I'm intrigued," he said, pulling lidded containers from the cooler. Homemade German potato salad, sauerkraut, pickles, chunks of bratwurst and sausages, two kinds of mustard, and a caesar salad kit still in the bag it came in.

"What a feast," Sarah exclaimed, pulling charcoal gray plates from her cupboard and silverware from a drawer. "I have a few more cans of Guinness or a German riesling."

"I'll have whatever you're having."

Sarah handed Jared some serving utensils before she grabbed the corkscrew and two glasses and carried things into her dining room. They made a couple of trips back and forth before everything was on the table. Jared opened one last container and showed Sarah that it contained cut up chicken breast, sweet potato, and some blueberries. "Is this okay?"

"Absolutely. He eats better than many humans. Thank you."

Jared grinned and said, "Here, boy," before setting the bowl on the floor next to his chair and sitting.

Whiskey inhaled his food before Jared and Sarah had put any of theirs on their plates. He hit Jared's leg with his paw as if to say, "Hey, my bowl is empty."

Jared laughed. "You ate it all. That's all there was." He ruffled Whiskey's neck fur. "It's all gone. I'll bring more the next time I come visit. I promise."

Whiskey slurped Jared's hand and then spun around twice on the dining room rug before curling into a ball next to Jared's chair.

"So, tell me all about this mystery," Jared said, before shoveling a forkful of potato salad into his mouth.

Sarah finished tossing the salad in a wood bowl and then put some on her plate next to all of the savory goodness. "You really put together quite a spread."

"Nothing is too good for mi'lady." Jared paused, before adding, "and my mutt."

Sarah laughed. "I hope he didn't hear you. I don't think he'd want to be referred to as a mutt, with its negative connotations and all."

"I'm sure." Jared speared a piece of bockwurst, popped it in his mouth, and chewed it thoughtfully. "Mmm. That bockwurst is delicious with that grainy mustard."

"I'll try it," Sarah said, stabbing a piece of it with her fork and dunking it into the seedy, golden condiment. She closed her eyes as she chewed. "Smoky with paprika. Did you see if it was made with pork or veal?"

"I didn't. Why?"

"I don't eat veal. The whole process seems inhumane."

"I don't either, but to be honest, I never even considered that the sausages could be veal."

"It's okay," Sarah said. "These are delicious, and I'll just stay ignorant since there's nothing we can do about the young cow's life now."

Jared's eyes sparkled at her from across the table. "Back to the mystery. Fill me in."

Sarah reminded him about her and Gladys finding Daisy and Donovan, how sick they were, and how Donovan was put into a coma. She said she didn't know if he had been released yet. She took a sip of wine and then texted Gladys to see if she knew.

Gladys' response was prompt. "The hospital decided to keep Donovan one more night until they could decide what made Cherie sick." Sarah read that and then told Jared about Cherie getting sick and Candace's visit to the Coiffure with the bunny and the revelation that cyanide was the cause of the illnesses. "Well, at least what was wrong with Daisy and Donovan," Sarah added.

Jared cut in, "But you suspect that's what they will find in Cherie's system too?"

Sarah nodded and took another sip of wine.

"Cyanide. It's like something out of James Bond or the suicide pills Hitler and his cronies took. Why would they ingest cyanide and how?"

Sarah pointed her fork at Jared. "That's what I'm hoping you and I will figure out." Sarah reached for her laptop that was sitting closed at the head of her table just as Jared pulled his phone from his pocket.

"I'll race you to find out what cyanide is, what its modern uses are, and where it's found." He grinned at her.

"Wait, that's three things. Does the race end when we've found all three or just one of them? Your challenge is unclear so I can't accept it. And why don't we search together?" She moved her chair toward him and angled her computer so they could both see the screen. Then she typed "cyanide" into the search bar.

Jared mumbled aloud some of the results. "First used in World War One. Found in car exhaust, cigarette smoke, and foods, such as spinach. Maybe that's why Popeye was weirdly shaped."

"Very funny," Sarah said. "So it says there are multiple kinds of cyanide, some with hydrogen, some with sodium or potassium, and others. I wonder which they ingested."

"Are you sure they ingested it? It's been used as a gas, I think, in times of war."

"Yeah well, there isn't a war in Cottageville that I know of. I don't think it's flying around on a breeze here. So for me, it makes most sense that they drank it or ate it."

"Okay, but can it be added to soap or shampoo or something and get into a person's system that way?"

"No idea," Sarah said. "But if it was in the soap or shampoo, you'd think Daisy would have gotten sick again after going back home."

"I agree that that makes sense, but I don't want to rule out any possibilities before we understand what all of them are." He forked some romaine lettuce into his mouth and chewed while staring at

Sarah's computer screen.

After he swallowed, he pointed to an article. "It says here that cyanide has legit uses in making paper, textiles, and plastics, and it is used as part of the chemicals when developing film—"

Sarah cut him off. "Who develops film anymore?"

"Enthusiasts. But I agree, not many people. It also says cyanide is used in electroplating, metal cleaning, and in gas form it is used to exterminate pests. You didn't see any bait boxes or anything like that around their property did you?"

Sarah's eyes were huge. "Are you kidding? With all of those dogs? Not a chance they'd use anything toxic like that." Then she remembered Daisy's words. "When Donovan first got sick he threw up by the barn. Daisy was so quick to clean it up as she didn't want the dogs eating the vomit in case it would make them sick, too. They love those dogs. They'd never put them in harm's way."

"Okay, okay. Then that brings us back to the food and beverage ideas."

"Cyanide is naturally in foods, but it seems like a person would need to eat a huge amount of spinach or almonds or whatever to ingest an amount of cyanide that would be poisonous." Sarah stabbed a lettuce piece but then eyed it suspiciously before returning it to her plate uneaten. She ate a forkful of sauerkraut instead. After swallowing, she asked, "Cabbage and carrots weren't on that list, right?"

"No, and even if they were, we haven't eaten enough of them to do any damage..." Jared's voice trailed off like he had wandered from their discussion into his head.

Sarah ate a bit more sausage and waited him out. Whiskey

snored from the floor near Jared's feet.

"Unless," Jared continued his earlier thought, "unless someone tampered with the food. Or water source at Donovan and Daisy's. Are they on city water or on a well, do you know?"

"No idea. But using my powers of deduction—god, I sound like a superhero—I would reason that their water wasn't tampered with. If it had been, the dogs and their other animals, them, Gladys and Bill, and maybe even Whiskey would all be dead. I didn't include myself because I don't remember if I had any water while I was there."

"Excellent points, Super Sarah. So that then brings us to food."

"When I visited Daisy in the hospital, she said they had gotten sick after lunch. I'm trying to remember what they ate. I think she said chicken from the night before that she cut into sandwiches on bread she made and an apple, or something like that."

Jared's forehead creased as he squinted at his phone's tiny screen as he typed something. "Apple seeds contain cyanide."

"Yeah, but one or two seeds isn't enough to send someone into a coma."

Jared typed some more and then said, "You're right, according to Google, and the CDC."

"I feel like we're still missing something." Sarah sighed. "And it's frustrating when we can't figure things out. I mean, I don't even really know Daisy and Donovan, but they seem like such nice people, and they love animals so much. Anyone who loves animals as much as they do has to be good, right?"

"You'd think. Especially since animals, particularly dogs, are better judges of people than people are sometimes."

"So true," Sarah said, pushing her plate away from herself. She drank the final sip of wine in her glass.

"Do you know what the police think?"

"Other than Candace saying they think it's suspicious and they are investigating, I don't. I mean, what does investigating mean in this sense? Are they testing their water and the stuff in their fridge? And why didn't Daisy get sick this time?"

Jared's eyes bore into Sarah's. "You said Daisy said she and Donovan had eaten lunch before they got sick."

"Yes. And she said after she put him to bed with a vomit bucket next to him, she made herself a cup of tea."

"But Donovan was already sick and didn't drink the tea?"

Sarah shook her head no.

"I don't even know if she drank it. All I remember is she said she made it and then started to feel sick and hurried just in time to the bathroom before she started to heave."

"So it had to be something with the food."

"I guess. But if Cherie got sick after eating, it wouldn't have been the same food. That was almost two weeks ago. Chicken, bread, they don't last that long."

"Unless they were frozen."

"Oh my!" Sarah exclaimed, her fingers tap, tap, tapping on her keyboard keys. "Bingo! See here." She put her index finger to the screen. "North Dakota State University's agriculture department says that frost and freezing causes plant cells to rupture and this can release cyanide. I mean, it is talking about the cyanide inherent in plants like sorghum and things and how this can poison livestock, but couldn't it do the same thing to humans?"

"Maybe, probably, I mean chemistry and biology weren't exactly my best subjects." Jared smiled and shrugged.

"Oh yeah, art guy. I remember."

"Exactly, but what you're saying seems logical if you're implying that whatever food contained cyanide—either naturally or otherwise—could have gone into the freezer and the freezing process could have caused those cells to rupture and make it worse." Jared picked up the wine bottle and offered Sarah a splash.

"I'm good," she said. "That is what I was saying but whatever food item we are talking about must have been eaten only by Cherie and not by Daisy. It's the only thing that makes sense."

"I agree." Jared stood up with his empty plate and walked to the kitchen with Whiskey as his shadow.

Sarah heard the dishwasher door open.

"Okay to put these in here?"

"Yes," Sarah said, gathering up her own plate and some of the containers of leftovers and carrying them into the kitchen.

"I know we aren't done talking," Jared stood up from the dishwasher and reached his hands over his head toward the ceiling. "But I was tired of sitting."

"I get it. Let's clean this up and take Whiskey for a walk just up to the park and back."

"Sounds good," Jared said, returning to the living room for the empty wine bottle and the remaining food items.

CHAPTER EIGHTEEN

arkness had descended since it was a new moon night as Jared, Sarah, and Whiskey got to the top of Sarah's street. A rustle of something in a rhododendron caught Whiskey's attention. He paused before the plant for a split second before taking off after a critter Sarah hadn't seen. His ears were back, his snout was extended, and his paws pounded the pavement until he hit the grass of the park. Jared and Sarah ran after him.

Sarah shouted, "Whiskey, come back here." She was glad she put her sneakers on instead of her flip flops.

"Whiskey, stop!" Jared yelled.

But Whiskey kept going.

He ran directly through the center of the park, and then he took a right on the sidewalk flanking Main Street.

Jared's breath was coming in gasps, and he put a hand to his right side. "Side stitch," he exhaled.

Sarah glanced at him, and realized sweat beads had started to form on his forehead. "You can stop here. I'll go get him." She took off after Whiskey again, leaving Jared bent over and breathing hard and audibly on the sidewalk.

"Come on, Whiskey. Stop chasing that thing."

He ran a few more feet, looked right and then left, and then turned his head back at Sarah.

When she caught up to where he had stopped, she found they were standing in the parking lot of the hospital, and that Daisy was walking through the sparsely filled space. Her head was down, and she was walking fast toward a minivan.

"Daisy," Sarah yelled, even though her breathing was a bit ragged from the chase. She and Whiskey jogged toward Daisy.

Daisy picked up her head and looked in Sarah's direction. "Oh. Hi. I didn't expect to see you here." When Whiskey got to her, she bent to pet him.

Once Sarah reached them, she said, "How's Donovan? And how's your friend? Gladys told me what happened."

"They are both well now, and I think they will both be released tomorrow."

"That's great news. Does that mean the police determined where the cyanide came from?"

Daisy's eyes widened like she was surprised Sarah knew

that detail. So Sarah shrugged and said, "Small town. News travels faster than lightning."

Daisy nodded. "They are still looking. But they determined it isn't in our well."

Sarah wanted to say, "Of course not," but she didn't want to be rude. Instead she said, "I kind of love to solve mysteries and so does one of my friends. We had dinner tonight and spent a couple of hours looking up everything we could about cyanide. And we think it probably was in something you ate, but we don't know why or how it got there. And we don't think it was naturally in the food."

Daisy's eyes narrowed and she looked at the ground, but Sarah could tell she wasn't seeing anything. She was thinking. When she met Sarah's eyes, Daisy's blue eyes were wide open and her mouth was in the shape of an O. "The only thing Donovan and I ate before we got sick and then Cherie ate too was a banana nut cake from Java and Juice. I cut it into pieces and put it in the freezer when I got it, and we take some out when we need something sweet."

"Wait, what?" Sarah's heart rate increased like she was watching a scary part in a movie. Except it was real life. She knew Ginger would never add cyanide to a recipe. It wasn't possible. *But why were questionable things attaching themselves to her best friend's business? First Richard Clarkson and now possibly this? Were they connected somehow?*

Whiskey's head picked up and he barked once. Then he left Sarah and Daisy to get Jared who was walking across the far end of the lot toward them.

In the lights towering over the parking lot, Sarah could see that Jared was breathing more regularly. To Daisy, she said, "You got the cake from Java and Juice? And that's the only thing in common each of you consumed before you got sick?"

"The cake was a congratulatory gift from our neighbor for rescuing our five hundredth dog. He said he got it from Java and Juice."

"Five hundred dogs? Wow. And you found homes for all of them?"

"Yes. It's something we are super proud of." Daisy smiled.

"You should be. That's quite an accomplishment. But back to the cake, are you sure that's the only thing you all ate? And you're sure he said he got it at Java and Juice? Do you have any left?" Sarah was certain that even if the cake was baked at Java and Juice somewhere along the way the cyanide had to have been added—but after the purchase. She wondered if it was the neighbor with the poodles or a different neighbor.

"Yes, that food is the only thing we all have in common. I didn't join Cherie in having cake after dinner. After everything I've been through, I figured my immune system didn't need any sugar. And yes, there's still almost half of the cake left in the freezer."

Sarah pulled her phone from her back pocket and called Chief James. He answered on the second ring just as Jared and Whiskey made it to Daisy's minivan.

"Hello, Sarah."

"Hey, Chief. Long story short, but I think you need to check the banana nut cake in Daisy and Donovan's freezer. She's headed to her house now—" Sarah raised her eyebrows at Daisy, who gave her a single nod and unlocked the van. "I've been in the hospital parking lot talking to her and it's the only thing all three of them ate before the reactions started so I think that's where you'll find the poison."

Chief James took in an audible breath that Sarah could hear through the phone, and before he could speak, Sarah added, "And Chief, Daisy said it was a gift from their neighbor, and that he said he bought it at Java and Juice."

"Java and Juice, huh?" Chief James said. "We'll see about that. No way Ginger is going to add poison to...well...anything."

"Exactly," Sarah said.

"Thanks for calling, Sarah. Officer Beams is working tonight and he's on his way to Daisy's."

"Thank you, Chief. And please let me know what you find."

The chief didn't agree to that. Instead, he said, "Good night, Sarah," and he disconnected.

"Thanks, Sarah," Daisy said. "Sounds like I've got to get home." She sat in the driver's seat and bid them goodnight.

Jared said, "Wow. Seems like I missed a lot, but I've got the gist of it. And there's no way we baked that cake. We make banana and nut muffins, and we add bananas to the smoothies. But in the five and a half years I've worked there, we've never made a banana nut cake."

"On Sunday, Ginger made pastries for a church group. Maybe she made one on a day the cafe was closed?" Sarah's voice rose at the end of the suggestion as she didn't even want to consider it as a possibility.

"I doubt it."

Sarah shrugged. "Since we're halfway between our places, if you want to go home instead of walking back with us, I understand. You've got an early morning."

"Thank you," Jared said, giving her a hug. "I'll get my cooler and containers another time. And tonight showed me that a) I've got to start jogging regularly. I'm so out of shape, and b) that Whiskey brought us where we needed to go again to help solve part of a mystery. I have no idea how he does that." He grinned down at the dog.

"I think this time it was a coincidence that he ran this far just as Daisy was leaving. I do wonder though, I mean, their neighbor was creepy in a way that didn't give me a good vibe, but to poison people…that's a whole different level."

"Yes, psychotic."

Sarah shivered though it was a very warm night.

"But don't think about that. Let's wait to hear what the police find. Are you sure you're okay to walk home by yourself?" Jared asked.

"I won't be. I'll walk with Whiskey," Sarah said, giving Jared one last hug. "Thank you for a fun evening. See you in the morning."

They parted and headed in opposite directions, and this time Whiskey walked by Sarah's side the whole way home with no distractions.

On the way to the Coiffure the next morning, Sarah and Whiskey ran into Candace Grimes, in uniform, just as they left Java and Juice. "Hey, Sarah. Whiskey," Officer Grimes said. "Thanks for last night's tip."

Sarah looked up and down the sidewalk before whispering, "Did it pan out?"

"Don't know yet," Candace said. "Following up a lead right now." She tilted her head toward Java and Juice.

"Ahh, makes sense. May your investigation go well and may you have a wonderful day," Sarah said. "And give Maple a kiss from me. Such a sweet guy."

Candace chuckled. "Sure thing."

When they were out of earshot of the cafe, Sarah said to Whiskey, "I bet she's following up on that cake, boy."

Whiskey trotted ahead of her but swished his tail in acknowledgment.

When they got to their green door, they found it open and Tony, in his usual gym shorts and tank top, and Spike were in the waiting area. Whiskey jumped and barked once at his friend, who barked and circled in response. Then they were off running under the counter and into the back room and back to Tony and Sarah, over and over like they were possessed by the zoomies. Sarah shut the door so they didn't dart through it and onto the street.

"How goes it, Big T?" Sarah asked.

"Fine, Sarah. Just fine. I hired a Pilates instructor, first time ever. You and Emily should come check it out. First class is on me." He grinned at Sarah and then at Emily who was behind the counter setting up the towel and shampoo and everything she'd need for Spike's bath.

"Pilates, huh? I figured your gym was about bulking up, not building long lean muscles and flexibility," Sarah joked.

"Gotta give the town a bit of both. I've been told that's what people want."

"Makes sense," Sarah said. "But you'll leave yoga to that woman who teaches at the Presbyterian church?"

Emily said, "You throwing shade, Sarah?" She grabbed Spike by the collar as he came past. "Into the tub you go, big boy. Whiskey, stay here and chill while your friend takes his bath."

Whiskey stood on his hind legs with his front paws atop the tub providing support for Spike.

Sarah set the bag from Java and Juice on the counter and then donned her denim paw print apron. "Not at all. Just figured Big T. needed to draw a line somewhere."

At Sarah, he flashed a friendly smile displaying bleached teeth. "I want to stay on brand," Tony said. "But when I ran numbers for adding Pilates equipment to a side room and calculated how many new members we could serve, I couldn't pass up the opportunity."

Emily added, "Oh, Tony, just admit it. If you have something trendy for mostly women, it could bring in more men, too. At least those who want that kind of eye candy." She laughed at her comment.

Pink tinged Tony's cheeks. "It was a solid business decision," he insisted.

"If women bring in more hetero men, that *is* a solid business decision," Emily said, wetting all of Spike's short fur with the hose.

Spike's jowls looked pouty and his eyes appeared sad. Baths were one of his least favorite things. Whiskey reached out a paw to try to touch him.

"Anyway," Sarah said. "Thank you so much for inviting us to try the Pilates class. Is it offered on the weekend?"

"Tuesdays, Thursdays, and Saturdays, at two. You can sign up on the website."

"I'll check it out," Sarah said.

"I'll be back in a few hours. Thanks. Bye, Spike. Be good." Tony left the Coiffure.

Sarah started to tell Emily about everything that happened since they saw each other last, but Ginger threw open the Coiffure's door. Though she looked adorable with her hair in two braids and wearing a lime t-shirt and white twill overalls, her face projected anger like a bull charging a red cape. "Why? Why? Why are people trying to destroy my business? What the hell is wrong with people?"

Sarah opened the counter and advanced toward her BFF. "I'm not trying to minimize your pain or anger, but I don't think it's personal. I mean, I don't think you or Java and Juice are being intentionally targeted. I think this last thing was using you out of convenience." She reached for Ginger's arm and pulled her down to sit on the sofa next to Sarah.

Ginger's eyes met hers and tears filled them.

"Oh, Ging. I understand how frustrating this is. First,

Dick, and now this poisoning."

"Dick definitely targeted us." Ginger wiped at her left eye with her left hand.

"Maybe, or he just carries the stuff around wherever he goes and takes advantage of what he sees as an opportunity. We don't know for sure."

"He sucks. And so does this neighbor of Daisy's, whoever he is. And before you ask, no, I've never made and sold a banana walnut cake at Java and Juice, not on my own nor for a special order. That's what I told Candace Grimes, too."

"That was basically what Jared told me last night," Sarah said. "And you are right, both men suck. But both will also get theirs."

"I don't want to wait as long as karma could take," Ginger said, wiping her other eye.

Must be waterproof, Sarah thought. *Ginger wasn't turning into a raccoon.*

"We won't have to wait for that. Chief James was getting a warrant, I believe."

"Lotta good it will do since Dick doesn't live here."

Sarah squinted her eyes at Ginger and said, "Babe, I believe if a warrant is issued, his local police will pick him up. And once all of those other defrauded restaurants and cafes get their lawyers on this, Richard Clarkson may be facing up to two dozen cases of fraud and whatever other charges they think will stick."

"He'd better," Ginger said. She glanced at her smart watch. "I've gotta get back. We had a lull, and I couldn't take being there any more. Thank you for listening to me. You're the best."

Sarah hugged her. "Any time."

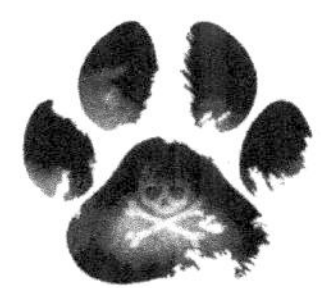

CHAPTER NINETEEN

The rest of the day flew by as Emily and Sarah washed and groomed six more dogs after Spike, clipped the nails on three drop-ins, and answered questions about price and service from an older woman named Celeste Ingram who had bleached hair, a t-shirt with sequins, and cropped cotton pants. She explained she had moved to town last week because she liked its quaint and safe energy. She introduced Emily, Sarah, and Whiskey to her timid maltese named Sunshine. The dog's hair was show-dog length to her feet but matted and gray at the ends from dragging in the dirt.

Sarah took pity on Sunshine and squeezed her into their schedule for the next morning. *No dog should ever be that dirty and tangled,*

Sarah thought. She felt it affected the dog's self esteem, and she was certain that if Sunshine had a shiny, slightly shorter, knot-free coat, and a bow on her head that she would act more confident.

At five o'clock, Emily swept the dog hair from the floor while Sarah refilled shampoo bottles and pulled the freshly laundered towels from the dryer and folded them for tomorrow. Whiskey napped near the sofa in the front room as he had exhausted himself playing with Spike and caring for every dog who walked through the door.

"Any plans for tonight?" Sarah asked.

"Just studying," Emily said.

"One of the T's or actual school work?" Sarah joked.

"Very funny. Not." Emily untied her apron and hung it from a hook and grabbed her backpack from where it was stashed in the back room. "I have a final on Friday. It's the last day of the summer term."

"Oh. I'm sure you'll get an A, as usual." Sarah picked up her empty to-go tumbler and her house keys. "Whiskey, time to go."

"I'd better get an A," Emily said. "I've been helping way too many of my classmates through this course. It's stats and it kind of sucks as I don't think the prof is awesome."

"That's too bad." Sarah locked up the Coiffure.

Emily got into her Honda, started it, and put down all of the windows. "I'll see you in the morning, Sarah."

"Have a good night, Em. Thank you for everything you do."

"You're welcome." Emily reversed out of the parking space and started down the road as Sarah and Whiskey walked up the sidewalk toward the park. When they got past the playground, Whiskey took off from Sarah's side. Sarah saw Chief James—in shorts and an old

Iowa State Cy the Cardinal t-shirt so he was clearly off duty—lob the Chuckit! ball at least thirty feet, and Sascha went after it with Whiskey giving chase. Sarah wasn't sure if he was interested in the ball or running with his friend, and she figured either one was good. He'd sleep well that night.

"Sarah, good to see you." Chief James extended his hand for Sarah to shake.

"Good to see you, too."

"Barbara's hosting one of those in-home sales events tonight for her friends, so we decided to give them some space."

"Candles, lingerie, cookware?" Sarah asked.

"No idea. She made salad and little sandwiches with the crusts cut off and opened a lot of wine. So Sascha and I went out for a burger and beer. Well, she only had the burger. And here we are."

Sarah chuckled. "Sounds like a good evening so far to me."

The chief threw the ball again and both dogs ran side by side after it, tongues hanging from the sides of their mouths and joy pouring from their faces. "You and Ginger may be happy to know this afternoon I got a judge to sign off on an arrest warrant for Richard Clarkson."

Sarah felt a weight she didn't even realize she was carrying lift from her chest. She could suddenly breathe more deeply. "That's the best news today."

"Tomorrow we'll send that to the P.D. where he lives and we'll make sure he gets picked up. We also received two calls from lawyers who are representing restaurants on your list that he had already sued. They are interested in our evidence though the evidence in many of those cases is long gone."

"That's a shame, really," Sarah said as Sascha brought the ball back to her human and dropped it at his feet.

He snatched it back up with the Chuckit! stick and threw it again and both dogs booked after the orange and blue ball. "It takes a lot to tire her."

"Him, too. Hey, when we were brainstorming about Richard Clarkson's scheme, we wondered if he got the allergens from where he worked. Specifically, we wondered if he may have stolen the vials."

Chief James pursed his lips and a v formed between his brows. "That's a good question, Sarah. We need to follow up on that." He pulled out his phone and made a note.

"I hate to think the worst of someone, but also, I want him to understand that when he tried to hoodwinked people in Cottageville, he messed with the wrong people. We protect our own and we don't take kindly to liars, cheats, and defrauders."

Chief James smiled. "It's true. And I like your passion."

Sascha and Whiskey returned again but this time Sascha allowed Whiskey to carry the ball. He dropped it on the chief's tennis shoe and then he lay on the ground next to the ball and shoe. His tongue protruded from his mouth and he panted.

"I guess he's done." Sarah chuckled as Sascha circled them once and then laid down next to Whiskey.

At that moment the chief's phone rang. "Order," he answered. "Uh huh. Okay. I'm on my way. Thanks, John."

The chief eyed Sarah for a moment and then said, "Officer Beams is bringing in the poodle breeder who lives next door to the couple that got sick."

"WHAT?! That was fast."

"I know. We still haven't heard from the lab on that cake, but I sent Beams to question him since he gave them the cake."

"Did he say why he tried to poison them?" Sarah felt like she was in an alternate universe. Dog lovers didn't try to poison one another. What was the world coming to?

"I know little. But I'm headed to the station. Good running into you, Sarah. Have a good night. Come on, Sascha. Let's go."

The German shepherd stood and followed the chief. Whiskey stood and wistfully watched her go before Sarah said, "Come on, boy, let's go home and get some dinner." He perked up at the word 'dinner' and displayed renewed vigor by speed walking toward home.

Sarah broke into a light jog to keep up, laughing as she went. "You're so funny, Whiskey. All you need to hear is the word food and you get a second wind."

He glanced over his shoulder at her and grinned.

After he ate a can of salmon and sweet potato dog food, Whiskey stretched himself out on the living room sofa and went to sleep. Sarah flicked through the choices on her streaming service for something to watch while she shoveled creamy gourmet mac and cheese that was previously frozen into her mouth. She had nuked it as opposed to baking it, so it wasn't as good as it could be. It lacked the crunchy bits that formed from cooking it for forty-five minutes in the toaster oven. But she was tired and hungry and didn't want to wait that long.

She stopped on the show of a cat behaviorist and watched a thirty-minute episode. "Geez, he has to deal with questionably behaving people as much as questionably behaving cats. I'd find that exhausting,"

Sarah said to Whiskey, who didn't even open an eye.

When the container of mac and cheese had been eaten, Sarah recycled the packaging and washed her fork by hand. Her phone chimed with an incoming text. It was Gladys, asking if she could call.

In response, Sarah called her.

"Sarah, I hope I'm not disturbing you, dear. But I wanted you to know that Donovan came home today and Cherie was released from the hospital, too."

"That's such good news, Gladys. How are they doing?"

"Daisy said Donovan has lost a lot of weight and he's weaker than he was, but the doctors think he'll make a full recovery. It's a miracle, I think."

"I think so, too. Did you know the police took their neighbor in for questioning, you know that awful man that I talked to after the ambulance took them away?" Sarah put some water on heat for tea.

"Oh my. I had no idea. Do you think Daisy knows? She didn't mention it."

"I don't know. But she'd have to suspect it was coming. I mean, I saw her last night and that's when we realized it was cake from the neighbor that probably made them all sick. Though he said the cake came from Java and Juice."

"Ginger would never do that. Oh dear. What a horrible man."

"I saw Chief James and Sascha in the park on the way home tonight. We stopped and talked when Officer Beams called to say he was bringing him in. That's the only reason I know." Sarah chose a bag of chamomile and blueberry tea and put it in her favorite red heeler mug while waiting for the water to reach the boiling point.

"I just can't believe anyone would do something like that to anyone else, especially next door neighbors. Neighbors should look out for each other."

Sarah could almost hear Gladys' head shaking. "I agree," she said. "Thank you so much for calling to let me know that Donovan and Cherie are out of the hospital. I'm sure Daisy is relieved. How are you and your girls doing tonight?"

"We are fine, dear. Bill was with us for supper and now he's actually out back cutting me a bouquet from my rose bushes. He's such a sweet man, Sarah."

"He is indeed, Gladys."

"Oh, he's coming back in. I'll let you go. Have a good night, dear."

"You too." Sarah disconnected and then she sent a group text to Jared and Ginger. It said, "Ran into Chief. Judge signed arrest warrant for Dick." She added a cop, chains, and the scales of justice emojis.

Ginger responded immediately. "Daniel says party at his place as soon as Dick's in the slammer."

"Sounds good to me," Sarah texted.

CHAPTER TWENTY

The next morning when Sarah and Whiskey walked through the red door of Java and Juice they found the place packed. Barbara and her best friend and mayor Trish sat by the door and they called Sarah over to their table as Whiskey practically jogged to Jared behind the counter.

"Whiskey, don't go back there," Sarah yelled over the din of the cafe.

"Hey, we heard you unraveled another mystery," Trish said. "There's a rumor that the poodle rescuers' neighbor confessed."

"Yeah," Barbara, whose hair was a brighter shade of blond than usual, said, "James jokes that he needs to make you an auxiliary member of the force."

"That's funny," Sarah said, looking around the room. Every single table was filled, almost to overflowing. "Are they giving something away this morning?" She moved her hand in a circular motion in front of her referring to all of the patrons.

Barbara shrugged.

Trish said, "Babs here may have spread the word that Java and Juice came under attack and needed our support. She's a saint that way."

Sarah's eyes grew big. "Wow. That was so nice of you."

"Hey, we need to make sure Ginger has enough money to fight that lawsuit. Plus," Barbara's voice dropped lower so others wouldn't overhead, "Ginger needs to know we all have her back. Always. No one around here would ever believe she'd poison someone."

"That's so sweet. And yes, we do have her back. The idea of her poisoning anyone is ludicrous," Sarah agreed.

"Besides." Trish held up her coffee cup. "This place has the best coffee, pastries, and salads in town."

"Indeed, it does," Sarah said. "And the best homemade dog biscuits. Speaking of which, I need to go stop Whiskey from eating too many. You ladies have a fabulous day."

"Thank you, Sarah," Barbara and Trish said in unison.

When Sarah got to the counter, she found Whiskey on the serving side, sitting next to Jared's feet. "Dog, I'm pretty sure a health inspector would not like finding you there."

"Mi'lady," Jared said. "May I have your go-cup?"

Sarah handed her tumbler across the counter and she eyed the pastry case. "Umm, surprise me with something and throw in one for

Em. And, you can choose our lunch salads, too. My brain needs a break after these last few weeks of research and intrigue."

Jared laughed. "I'm sure. It's tough work being a sleuth on top of your day job. Even with the assistance of your gallant and humble servant." He bowed at the waist. "I did mean me, not Whiskey, mi'lady."

Sarah cracked up. "Of course and more like you are Robin to my Batman or Watson to Sherlock."

"I'd prefer the latter to the former." Jared put the food he had picked for her into a Java and Juice bag, told her the total, and handed her the bag and her tumbler.

"Thank you, Jared. Come on, Whiskey, let's go."

Whiskey ran from around the counter and wove between the tables to the door where he waited for her to catch up.

When they got to the Coiffure, they opened the door to find a bouquet of yellow roses, baby's breath, and pink carnations in a clear vase on the counter. "Wow, those are gorgeous," Sarah said. "Which T got you flowers?"

Emily was placing towels next to washbasins and setting up everything they would need for the day. Her blue tipped hair was spiky and the t-shirt under her dog print apron matched her hair's hue. She wore black stretchy pants and black combat boots on her bottom half. "Neither. Those are for you, not me. Daisy was here not more than two minutes ago. You just missed her. I think she said there's a card."

Sarah placed her tumbler and the bag of the food on the counter next to flowers. She pulled the note from the plastic holder stuck amongst the flowers.

A small gesture to say thank you for your kind and grand gesture of saving our lives. —Donovan and Daisy

"Wow. That was so sweet." Sarah's eyes filled with tears. "I wasn't looking for appreciation. I did what anyone would do in that situation."

"Not everyone," Emily said. "Clearly their neighbor wouldn't have, based on the rumors floating around town."

Sarah wiped her right eye with her right hand. "Point taken. It's just that they are so nice. I'm so glad they are going to be okay."

"Me, too," Emily said. "Now, about today's schedule. We have three bigger dogs, two medium size ones, and one ornery Chihuahua coming in. How do you want to divide the workload?"

Sarah was grabbing her apron and started to answer when the green front door opened and the first of the big dogs, a fluffy whitish great Pyrenees named Pedro led his tiny elfin-looking human into the waiting area. Kirsten Powers couldn't have been taller than four-foot-eleven—and she was a size zero Sarah was certain—but the smile on her face was as big as her dog. "Sarah, Emily. So good to see you again."

Whiskey dropped the rawhide he had been gnawing near the sofa to welcome his oversized and gentle friend.

"Good to see you, too," Sarah said. She reached for Pedro's leash and opened the counter top to lead him into the washing area. "We will have him done by late morning, if that fits your schedule."

Kirsten nodded and said, "I'm showing some houses to potential buyers this morning. I'll swing by as soon as I'm done."

"Sounds good," Sarah said, "and may you be able to write up an offer."

Kirsten grinned again. "That's the plan. Thank you. Bye, Pedro. I'll see you after your bath, my love." She blew him a kiss and then walked out the door.

"I'll take care of Pedro, Em. You get the dog that walks through the door next."

Pedro willingly stepped into the basin, and Sarah was certain it would be a good day.

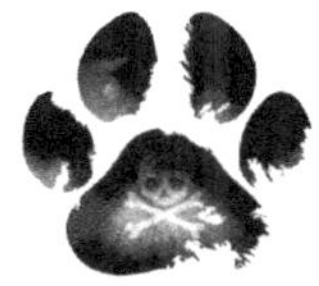

EPILOGUE

Over the next few weeks, Donovan gained weight and strength as he and Daisy ate healthy foods and worked as much as he was able to around their farm. And it was a good thing he had most of his stamina back, because when their neighbor got arrested and charged with attempted murder of them plus the additional charges of endangering Cherie, his poodles were left all alone. The man's wife had run off years ago and he had no children nor any relatives to care for them or his property.

Daisy, being the kind soul that she was, offered to take the dogs and care for them, even though Chief James made it clear to her that with the charges their attempted murderer was facing he wouldn't outlive his probable sentencing or see the dogs again.

"It's okay," she assured him. "They shouldn't suffer because of his horrible deeds."

"You're a caring and excellent human," Chief James said.

When the neighbor confessed to Officer Beams, his rage ran from him like a river after torrential rains. He cursed Daisy and Donovan for ruining his poodle breeding business by "undercutting his prices by offering sub-rate dogs of suspect lineage." He claimed, year by year they had whittled away his business and showed no remorse for his suffering and no respect for his superior bloodlines.

When Chief James read the interview notes, he looked up and asked, "He is talking about the dogs, right? That last line could be mistaken for skinhead speech."

Beams sat across the desk from the chief and said, "Yes, it was about the dogs and how they were willing to rescue poodles and any other types of dogs, including ones that would need a DNA test to prove their heritage. He hated that they treated all dogs equally."

"Wow," Chief James said.

Beams nodded his head. "I know."

"Did he say where he got the cyanide?"

"It took me a while to get him to talk about that but you'll see it further down in the interview. It's rather inventive and scary. He read online that stone fruit and cherry pits and apple seeds and a number of other foods naturally contain cyanide, so he started saving them up as he ate those things. Then, once he had enough, he ground them down into a kind of flour, and he used that to make the cake."

"That'd take quite a bit, as seeds are small."

"Yep. Said he got the idea a year ago and has been planning since."

"That's a lot of hate and completely bonkers. You think his lawyer is going to try to talk him into pleading insane?"

"No idea. At least no one died and we figured it out."

"Yes, with Sarah's help."

Beams grinned. "She's got a mind for mysteries and their solutions."

"Speaking of which, did you hear Richard Clarkson's place of employment ended their own investigation and found he'd altered the inventory files for years to conceal his theft of the shellfish allergen? He left a digital footprint and they located video surveillance footage of him pocketing some vials. He's been fired and they have pressed charges."

"Does Ginger know?" Beams asked.

"I'm not sure. But let's go tell her." Chief James stood and walked to the door of his office and Beams followed him.

They walked a few blocks to Java and Juice and found Ginger and Jared behind the counter and Whiskey and Sarah in front of the counter placing a lunch order. Sarah turned when she heard the bell over the door tinkle. Whiskey ran to greet them, and one at a time they patted his head.

"Chief. Officer Beams. Good to see you both," she said. Her coppery hair was in a high ponytail and her work apron covered her clothes.

The chief looked around the cafe and waved at the Parks and at his wife who was in bright blue yoga clothes and was eating lunch after class with Trish. "Hi, honey. Good afternoon, mayor," he said.

Barbara blew him a kiss but kept up her conversation. Trish McGowan briefly shifted her eyes from Barbara to her husband and said, "Chief," as Barbara kept talking.

The chief and Beams approached the counter. Sarah stepped aside to give them some room.

Jared handed Sarah a bag with two salads and two cookies. "Thanks, my lord," she said.

"My pleasure, mi'lady."

Beams shook his head in amusement. "You two crack me up."

"What can I get you, Chief?" Ginger asked.

"Coffee. Black. But we came by to let you know that Richard Clarkson may be going away for a long time." He recapped the pharmaceutical company investigation and charges and mentioned at least two jurisdictions besides theirs had issued arrest warrants.

Ginger grinned. "And I heard this morning that all nineteen of the restaurants that he won lawsuits against are suing him. They want their money back and they're suing for damages to their reputations, too."

"Good. I'm glad they were able to use the information we provided," Sarah said.

"Yes, the information you and Whiskey discovered," Officer Beams added.

Sarah's smile stretched wide. "You hear that Whiskey? You found that orange and helped uncover a fraudster. Maybe Chief James should give you a badge."

"Uhh, Sascha might have something to say about that if she doesn't get one too," the chief joked.

"I haven't seen her out in town solving any crimes," Sarah said, "but she's welcome to join us any time."

"I'll keep that in mind, Sarah, I'll keep that in mind."

Ginger handed a black coffee in a takeaway cup to the chief and a mocha to Officer Beams, who claimed he needed some sugar as an afternoon pick-me-up. When the chief tried to pay, Ginger told him they were on the house and any food they wanted, too. "I'm glad we can all work so well together to keep our community safe," she said as she lifted her own coffee mug in salute.

"To us," said Jared, lifting his bottle of water.

"To us," Sarah agreed.

And Whiskey must have sensed the happiness of the humans because he jumped up and barked and then flashed his black gummed grin.

Sarah's heart felt full of love for her friends and especially for her beautiful red heeler Whiskey. Her furry personal super hero.

Want more Whiskey the Cattle Dog Mysteries? Read a sneak preview of book three in the series, *Canines and Candy Canes*, which will be released in time for the holidays in 2024. To sign up to receive sneak previews and release dates about other books in the Whiskey Dog Mystery Series, go to https://www. whiskeydogmysteries.com

CANINES
AND
CANDY CANES

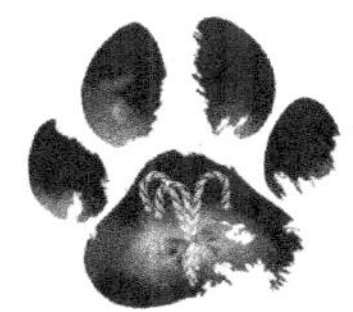

CHAPTER 1

"Are you sure you can fit me in?" Sarah Carter, the twenty-eight-year-old proprietor of Carter's Canine Coiffure, asked Jared Greene, her friend, occasional date, the best barista in Cottageville, and graphic artist extraordinaire.

"Of course I can fit you in. I told you I'd meet you at the Coiffure on Sunday morning at ten." Jared didn't look at Sarah as he said those words. He was focused on the library's big plate glass windows. Ever since he had gotten off work from Java and Juice at two p.m., he had been at the library. He hadn't been looking for books. He had been climbing up and down a ladder painting an outline of the holiday scene that Carole Binds, the head librarian, asked him to create "to bring some secular Christmas joy" as she called it to one of the community's primary meeting places.

In fact, once word got out that Jared had sold his first graphic novel to a major New York publisher, the residents of Cottageville had started to look at him differently. No longer was he the six-foot-three auburn-haired coffee and croissant server at the most popular cafe in town. Suddenly he was an Artist, with a capital A, who just happened to enable their morning caffeine fixes.

And because of that shift in perspective, Jared was in demand to create holiday renderings on all of the windows of all of the businesses in town. So far he had painted children on sleds zipping down hills on the automatic doors of Cottageville Hospital's emergency room, oversized wrapped gifts and colorful candies on the every window of the elementary school, a hot cocoa and apres ski scene on the windows at Java and Juice, cartoon children whose faces were awash with wonder at their gifts on the windows of the toy store, and a Dalmatian with a red bow around its neck at the firehouse. Jared had worked seven days a week for fourteen hours a day for the whole month of November—between his two jobs—and it was now December first, and Sarah wondered if he was sick of painting.

"If you are tired of this..." Sarah's voice trailed off.

Despite the near freezing temperature, Jared wore a buffalo check plaid flannel shirt over a thermal Henley and jeans, as he couldn't paint big murals in a bulky coat and while wearing gloves. "Sarah," Jared said, finally looking at her.

She knew he was serious when he called her by name. Usually he joked and called her "mi'lady" in this whole silly chivarious schtick they did. "Yes, Jared?" she asked, holding his green-eyed gaze.

"I am tired. Very tired. But this is also super inspiring for me. I came to Cottageville more than six years ago because I knew it would be a place that would give me the freedom and space to make art. And look at me now. I have my first book coming out with a major publisher next year. And our fine neighbors are finally recognizing me for my talent beyond frothed milk and foam art. I'm living my dreams and I'm loving every minute of it."

Sarah grinned at him. "I'm sure. I am so glad you are finally being seen for you and everything you contribute to this town and our lives and...well...to the world. It's exciting. I'm glad to be on this journey with you. But I am worried you are wearing yourself too thin. That's why I don't want you to feel obligated—"

He cut her off with a red paint speckled index finger to her lips. "Shhh. I'm glad you care about me and for my well-being. But seriously, painting a dog on the door of your shop will take me like fifteen minutes. Twenty tops. I'm gonna paint a portrait of Whiskey with a big candy cane in his mouth."

Whiskey, Sarah's almost seven year old Australian red heeler cattle dog, whined when he heard his name. He rubbed against Jared's left leg. Jared was one of his most favorite people in a sea of favorite people in their town.

Jared reached down and ruffled his ears. "You're such a good boy. Yes, you are," he said.

When Jared looked up at Sarah again, he said, "And when I'm done, you can pay me by taking me to brunch." He grinned.

"Perfect," Sarah said. "I'll make a reservation at Poached Perfection for ten-thirty."

"Delightful." He kissed the end of her nose and then turned back to the library's windows. He picked up a container of green paint, pulled a brush from his back pocket, and climbed to the top of the ladder.

"Be careful up there," Sarah said to Jared, before addressing her dog. "Come on, Whiskey. Let's be on our way so Jared can work."

Like a grand marshal, Whiskey led the way up Main Street—though he stayed on the sidewalk—until they got to where the park began on the other side of the road. Whiskey set his butt on the snow-dusted pavement and waited until Cottageville's one street light turned green again, and it was safe for them to cross. Then, with his white-tipped tail in the air and a glance over his shoulder to make sure Sarah, wrapped in her navy blue winter jacket and multi-colored wool scarf, was following, he marched across the street and into the park's powdery snow topped grass where he promptly dropped to his side and rolled back and forth on his spine.

Laughter burst from Sarah at the canine version of a snow angel. "Does that feel good, boy?"

Whiskey wiggled his shoulders and butt forming c's and backwards c's before bouncing onto his four paws, shaking the dirt, grass, and snow from his coat, and resuming their walk. He followed the path that meandered through the park until he spied his friend Sascha, a German shepherd who lived with Cottageville Chief of Police James Order and his wife Barbara. Chief James held a lime green Chuckit! stick in one hand and flicked his wrist, which caused the orange and blue ball to go sailing. Like a greyhound after a rabbit, Sascha sprinted after the ball. And Whiskey took off after her.

Sarah jogged to keep up, but she felt more like the runt at the back of the pack. Sascha, with the ball in her mouth and Whiskey by her side, returned to Chief James before Sarah caught up to them. "Afternoon, Chief," she huffed.

"Sarah. Good to see you." He threw the ball again and the dogs took off. "Will you be at Winter Wonderland?"

Trish McGowan, Cottageville's mayor and Barbara Order's best friend since childhood, hosted a holiday event the first weekend in December every year. The festivities kicked off on Friday night when the mayor plugged in the hundreds of colorful lights wrapped around a majestic white pine, the tallest tree in Cottageville Park. Then she gave a speech of gratitude and accolades to citizens who had done amazing things for the town over the past twelve months. That was followed by a scavenger hunt for the children. For the whole weekend, local businesses set up booths of games, arts and crafts, food and drinks, and merchandise for sale to help people get into the Christmas spirit. And people from all over descended on Cottageville like Swifties at one of Taylor's concerts. This one weekend was the town's peak tourism time.

For the past six seasons, Carter's Canine Coiffure had set up a table selling Christmas, Hanukkah, and Kwanzaa-themed bandannas, collars, and leashes, as well as donating gift certificates and services for the silent auction. All of the money raised was donated to the local food pantry that fed more than three hundred families each week.

Sarah said, "Whiskey and I wouldn't miss it. We are sharing a big booth with Java and Juice this year as I talked Ginger into selling her homemade dog biscuits as well as her fabulous food for humans."

Ginger Jones owned Java and Juice, and when Sarah had moved to Cottageville more than six years ago, she and Ginger struck up a friendship that quickly turned them into BFFs.

"Oh that's great. We should get some for Sascha's stocking. She can't get enough of those biscuits." Sascha had "only child status" in her household. Chief James used the lime green thrower to pick up the saliva-slick ball she dropped at his feet. "You tired yet?" he asked his dog. Her tongue protruded from the right side of her mouth and she was panting. But her body tensed, ready to go after the ball another time.

Whiskey looked from Sascha to Chief James and then lined up his shorter legs and body next to hers, imitating her stance. As soon as the ball snapped from the holder, they took off, pounding the ground in syncopated rhythm.

"They're so fast," Sarah said. She admired the way their muscles moved causing their fur to ripple. Whiskey may have been more barrel shaped than Sascha, but his breed had been created for herding cattle and keeping them in line, and that took speed. He stayed neck and neck with his longer legged friend.

This time, Sascha let Whiskey snatch the ball in his jaws. He smiled around it and raced back toward Chief James with Sascha running as his wing woman. Whiskey dropped the ball below the laces on Chief James' black leather boot, and it rolled from there to the ground. Then Whiskey collapsed on his belly with his arms bent at the elbows like he was doing a sphinx pose in yoga class.

Looking down at him, Chief James chuckled. "I think we're done. Barbara is expecting us home for supper anyway. Come on,

Sascha. Nice seeing you, Sarah."

Whiskey stood and sniffed his friend's ear as a good-bye. Sascha stood stock-still and let him.

Chief James scratched Whiskey's forehead. "Thank you for playing with us, Whiskey."

"Thank you for permitting him to," Sarah said. "Let's go, boy." She motioned for Whiskey to walk the path with her. He stayed by her side as Sarah contemplated the contents of her fridge and what she could make for her supper.

They had gone twenty steps when a screech of tires cut through Sarah's thoughts. A loud BOOM followed and then half a second later, the shattering of glass pierced the chilled air. The three sounds happened so fast in succession that Sarah froze in shock.

"What the heck?" she said aloud. She turned and looked toward the park entrance where she saw Chief James running like he was trying to break a land speed record. Sascha sprinted beside him with ease.

In a split second decision, Sarah ran after them, toward the sound of the accident. Whiskey passed her when they were halfway across the park. His mouth was open and his tongue hung low. "Slow down, Whisk," Sarah panted.

Whiskey slammed on his brakes at the entrance, thumped his tail against the ground, and waited for her to catch up.

Lots of people—in various manners of dress—were now pouring onto Main Street. Some women wore aprons over their clothes, like they had been in the middle of cooking dinner. Jackets and appropriate winter attire were being pulled on and zipped as people raced from their residences and shops. None of them paid attention to Whiskey or Sarah. Their eyes were searching two blocks down Main Street, where the trailer end of a semi-truck could be seen at an almost jackknifed angle to the street, blocking traffic on both the north and southbound sides.

The truck's cab was crumpled. It had crashed through the big plate glass windows of Cottageville's pride and joy, its library.

Sarah couldn't see the ladder Jared had been standing on. And she couldn't see Jared.

Her heart slammed in her chest causing her to gasp.

"Jared!" Sarah screamed, before she ran faster than she ever had in her life, weaving between her neighbors and strangers, with Whiskey close on her heels.

Sign up to follow Faith Walker and to never miss another Whiskey Dog Mystery release. Go to http://www.whiskeydogmysteries.com or follow us on social media @whiskeydogmysteries.

www.ingramcontent.com/pod-product-compliance
Lightning Source LLC
Chambersburg PA
CBHW072009210726

48294CB00013B/1750